America is talking about
WHO WILL HEAR MY SCREAMS

W9-BXX-696

"I got chills."

"A real page-turner."

"I really got hooked."

"Love, hate, jealousy, obsession
and spine-tingling fear... all the
components of a master story
weaver."

"If Terry McMillan and Dean
Koontz wrote a book... This
would be it."

Who Will Hear My Screams

ANNA DENNIS

Apex Publishing

Who Will Hear My Screams

ISBN: 0-9706257-0-7

Printed in the United States of America

10 9 8 7 6 5 4 3 2

for
Merceal Swezey
My Loving Mother

I Thankfully Acknowledge...

GOD, for lest I build a house without Him, I labor in vain. I thank Him for this precious opportunity and gift and for allowing me to find favor in His eyes.

My husband, Edward Dennis, my best friend, support system, protector, provider and strength. You have always seen the bigger picture-thank you for helping me to realize it...I love you.

Ariana, my "Mini me." You'll always be my little angel and by far the greatest gift GOD could have ever afforded me.

My mother, Merceal Swezey, for all your sacrifices and constant love. And, for always knowing I could do whatever I set my mind to and helping me to attain it.

My grandmother, Ruthie Russell, my aunts Martha Robinson and Betty Tipton, for your prayers, guidance and mouth-watering, home-cooked meals that keep my roots firmly planted.

My grandfather, the late RC Russell, Sr. 'a.k.a.' "Daddy," for giving this family strong roots. I miss you.

My uncles, RC & Allen Russell, my father-in-law Edgar Dennis, Jr. and stepfather Darrell Swezey, for being constant, positive, male role models amongst a dying breed.

My sister, Monique Fleming, my niece LaCreshe Acevedo, my cousins, Tania Levingston, Leisa White and Tommy Frazier for giving me great character ideas. Michelle Shadden for hookin' me up...thanks, girl.

My editor, Fran Wessel for the wonderful job you did of bringing more clarity and depth to my work.

Jaylin, my graphic designer, for capturing my vision.

My friend, Jerry Thompson, for introducing me to the literary world and all the possibilities it has to offer.

My friend, Donna Hill for your support, inspiration, encouragement and time. Because you blazed the trail, I am here...

Who Will Hear My Screams

Chapter One

Mia Simone sat at the small, wooden table and massaged her cramping fingers. This evening she had signed more than sixty copies of her new, psychological thriller entitled, *A State of Mind*. Thinking back, this had been one of her more successful book signings. She could remember other signings where she had only been asked for two or three signatures by actual book buyers and sold even less. *A State of Mind* had done extremely well in its second life. It was originally published three years ago, but now in reprint and with a different title, people seemed to be ready for it. Mia chalked the former result up to being a book ahead of its time.

She pulled the DayTimer from her briefcase and looked at the weeks ahead. There were six more book signings scheduled for this month. She could hardly believe it; this was the career she had always dreamed of. Five years ago she had become fully vested at her job as editor for a popular magazine. Leaving behind the twelve to fourteen hour workdays and the ridiculous deadlines, she took the money from her 401k and had her husband invest it in some aggressive stocks that had produced nicely. Mia immediately began writing her first novel and completed it within five months. Bypassing the many rejection letters she had heard about while attending writer's group meetings, Mia opted to self-publish her book. She knew it was a risky move on her part and not really well respected in the writing industry, but she had confidence in her work. She had heard authors and agents alike say that self-published books seemed indicative of a person who had received many rejection letters, but never taken the time to find out why the book was being rejected. Therefore, there must be a problem with the book or just plain sloppy writing involved. Mia on the other hand begged to differ. She knew how to write and edit a story from the twelve years of working at the magazine company. She just didn't know the behind-the-scenes business of getting a book on the shelf versus getting a story to print in a magazine. In any event, the book had proven itself within six months of its release. *A State of Mind* had made several bestseller lists and had been optioned for a movie. By the time her book had been on the market for a year, she was being likened to some of the great psychological storytellers of her time.

Now, three years later, she was still enjoying the profits made from the book as a result of a large New York publisher purchasing the rights to do another run. Mia couldn't believe her success as a first time author, but she felt the time had come to do a sequel. She had done several short stories and an anthology during her three-year hiatus; however, none of them were as yet published. But now she was ready to spread her creative wings once again. She had worked with one very prominent psychologist to obtain most of her research and had remained in contact with her just in case she decided to do a sequel or other books, which would require some psychological background. The hardest part of writing the book had been keeping disciplined enough to write at a certain time each day, when she really didn't want to. She could easily fall prey to watching soap operas and talk shows during the day and reruns of sitcoms in the evening — all the things she had missed out during the years she was part of the hectic Los Angeles workforce. She zipped up her DayTimer and shoved it back in her briefcase. Suddenly, she felt a strong hand on her shoulder. The familiar, sensual squeeze sent a warm sensation throughout her.

"Hey Hon, you ready to go?" Mia looked over her

shoulder and up into her husband's handsome face. Edward Simone seemed to get sexier every year with his perfectly chiseled body, prominent features, long, dark lashes and alluring smile.

"I sure am. What do you say we get some Chinese food on the way home?"

"Sounds great," Edward said as he kissed his wife full on the lips.

"What was that for?"

"That was for being you and this is for having such a successful book signing this evening." He said, as he gathered her in his arms and kissed her passionately, his tongue probing knowingly inside her mouth.

"Hey, hey you two get a room!" came a voice from across the room. Lynda, the bookstore's owner entered as she pretended to cover her eyes. Mia had met Lynda eight years ago when the magazine she worked for did an article on Lynda's bookstore. It named her as one of the movers and shakers to watch for. Back then Mia was doing more interviewing than editing. She conducted the interview with Lynda and immediately liked her. They both shared the dream of managing their own business and their own schedules. They soon became fast friends and met weekly when Lynda started a writing group for local authors. Mia had many "so-called" friends in college that she kept in contact with until she got married, but Lynda had been her one true friend. She had been supportive in every way, no matter what Mia was going through, never once judging her. Many of her previous friendships had been plagued with jealousy, envy or what seemed to be the need to get close to her husband. Lynda Hastings was a strikingly, beautiful woman with no reason to be jealous or envious of any woman and since men flocked at her heels, she had absolutely no interest in Edward. Her arresting hazel eyes and shoulder-length, auburn hair, which she always wore in a tight bun, were attributes that made men drool. Mia could never understand why Lynda had never chose to settle down and marry, for she knew that it was not due to the lack of offers. Lynda's skin was the color of honey and so close to her hazel eye color that the comparison was startling. She had a gorgeous figure, with full breasts and buttocks that put Mia's to shame. Whenever Mia saw her, she always thought Lynda had missed her calling as a supermodel.

"You were a hit tonight," Lynda exclaimed. "The first thing on my list is to order more copies of your book tomorrow," Lynda continued, "It's hard to believe this book is three years old. One would think this was its first release. We even have twenty-five people on a waiting list. I can't thank you enough for squeezing my little book store into your busy schedule."

"Well now, that's what I like to hear and don't mention it. You were the one three years ago who got my name and face out there," Mia said excitedly.

"Yeah, you've come a long way from a three or four person audience to standing room only."

"Well, I'm just lucky. You know there's no way to anticipate how many people will attend a reading."

"Oh sure, that is of course, unless you're Mia Simone," Lynda offered.

"Stop it now before you make me blush," Mia feigned embarrassment.

"That's my Mia. I always told her she could do it," Edward interjected as he picked up Mia's briefcase and hefted it in his right hand. "I'll take this to the car and meet you out front. You take it easy Lynda."

"You too, Edward," Lynda replied as she watched Edward walk away. "You are one lucky woman, Mia. A handsome, caring husband who's a CFO. You couldn't have done better if you had dreamed him up," she said poking Mia in the arm with one of her perfectly manicured fingernails.

"I certainly am. I have a wonderful husband and

great people like you in my life." Mia said somewhat distracted.

"Is there something bothering you? You look upset," Lynda asked with growing concern.

"Oh nothing really. It's just that—" Mia paused as if unsure how to start. " I noticed this guy in the audience that I'm pretty sure I've seen at every one of my signings on this tour. It didn't bother me at first, but now—"

"What's wrong with that?" Lynda interrupted. "You have many fans of your work, Mia. Both men and women. I think that alone is a major accolade."

"I know, but there's just something about this guy that is just...creepy. He stays in the back during the readings and stares directly at me and then he disappears before the signing ends. Not to mention, on this first leg of the new tour, I've been to three different cities. I could see if I was Mariah Carey or somebody, but I'm not. I don't know, maybe it's nothing."

"Well, Hon, maybe it is nothing and maybe it's everything. You can't be too careful these days. I mean this book has really put you over the top and given you worldwide exposure. Unfortunately, you become exposed to the good and bad elements of the world. Have you mentioned this creep to Edward yet?

"No. You know how he is. He would overreact and have me doing readings from an interactive television or something." Both women laughed as they walked toward the front of the bookstore.

"Oh, and for the record," Lynda joked. "If you and Mariah were in the same room, *she* would definitely have something to worry about."

Mia and Edward sat in the family room of the their contemporary, four-bedroom, Spanish-style home in

Sherman Oaks, eating Chinese food and listening to soft jazz. She had changed into a pair of forest green, silk paja- mas and matching slippers, while Edward changed into his black silk pajama bottoms and robe, exposing his bronzed, bare chest. Mia loved these uninterrupted, intimate moments with her husband. They were few and far between given her hours spent writing, the boards she served on and Edward's long hours as CFO of the accounting firm he worked for. As they pushed aside the empty food containers and sat cuddled in front of the fireplace on the Persian rug, Edward stroked Mia's exposed belly, thumbing the baby- soft skin. He lowered his head to hers, placing a feather- light kiss on her lips. He stared at her and a smile formed at the corner of his lips.

"What are you smiling about?" Mia asked, prop- ping herself up on her elbows.

"You know you were a big hit tonight. I'm really proud of you. You're finally living your dream."

"Yeah, I know," Mia said as she stared absently into the crackling fire.

Edward tilted her chin to face him, concern in his eyes. "What's wrong? You look a million miles away."

Mia considered telling Edward about the weird guy in the audience. She had only *really* noticed his presence at the past few readings, but was sure he had been at every one. However, she couldn't understand why this time upset her so much. Maybe because of the way he seemed to leer at her— oblivious and unconcerned as to whether anyone might have been watching him. It had made Mia very uncomfortable, but she didn't want to alarm Edward—not yet anyway.

"I guess I was just thinking about how unbelievably blessed I am. I mean, ever since I was a little girl it has been my dream to write and now, I'm doing it. It's very hum- bling."

"It is definitely humbling, but it's also wonderful. I would imagine it's a lot like being famous. I mean people coming to see you that don't even know you. And, paying to read what you write about. But, I'm really the lucky one. I have you all to myself and I don't have to buy your book to know what you're talking about," Edward said with a seductive glint in his eye as he leaned over and kissed Mia full on the lips.

"You are the lucky one. I would charge you a lot more," she teased stroking the side of his handsome face. Edward laughed heartily.

"With my financial expertise, I could set up various portfolios for payment if it ever came down to that."

"That's okay. Your credit is good here."

"Just like I said, I am the lucky one."

The intimacy of the moment, the spicy food and good wine intensified the ambiance. Their bare feet brushed against each others intermittently, sending butterfly flurries throughout Mia's body. Edward began to slowly unbutton Mia's top. Her breath seemed to catch in her throat as it always had during the six years they had been married. He cupped her full breasts, massaging the nipples tenderly between his long fingers. Mia let out a sigh as her body shuddered at the urgent need deep within her. Edward lowered his head to suckle one of her breasts. A roaring fire began in her groin as the need to extinguish it became more than she could bear. Edward was an unselfish lover, allowing Mia to experience total pleasure during their lengthy foreplay.

Edward moved from her soft breasts to her smooth stomach and then around to the arch of her back, planting sensuous kisses along his travels. When Edward rolled her onto her back, Mia placed her arms around Edward's neck feeling the strong muscles in his taut shoulders and biceps. As he gingerly positioned himself atop her, with one hand he expertly removed her silk panties in one fluid movement.

Mia sighed again in anticipation of the long-awaited moment. As Edward entered her, he looked deep into her gray eyes...into her soul. His dark eyes conveying what she already knew...that he loved her more than anything. Mia whispered in Edward's ear, "I love you so much."

As Mia and Edward traveled on their rhythmic and explosive journey, the elements seemed to condone their love. The fireplace seemed to burn a little brighter as if blanketing their internal heat with its external warmth. The sun, which seemed to have been resting on the ocean only moments ago, had all but disappeared as if to quiet the atmosphere for only them. Slowly, Edward thrust himself deeper into Mia, his body fitting perfectly into the concavity of hers. The brief flash of pain gave way to a wondrous, familiar feeling that made her toes curl as she dug her fingernails into the firm, smooth flesh on his back. All that could be heard was their steady breathing and hushed whispers known only to lovers in the throes of passion. Time seemed to stand still for the enthralled lovers as Edward gathered Mia in his arms. His groans were muffled in her neck as he buried himself deeper within the confines of her heated walls. Together Edward and Mia found their shared rhythm that seemed to reach new heights. As Mia's sighs reached a crescendo, Edward placed his warm mouth over hers, devouring her full lips and muffling her sounds. He kneaded one of her firm, full breasts in his hand as he suckled the nipple like the sweetest fruit. His pace quickened and Mia held on wanting to take him all in, knowing the fantastic ride was coming to an end. As if awaiting her permission, Edward whispered her name, "Mia."

"Yes," she answered. Mia held fast and squeezed her eyes shut so tightly that tiny stars of light appeared. She imagined herself in space, weightless—on an exotic, unending journey where only promised pleasures lay ahead.

Chapter Two

Mia lay nestled in Edward's arms thinking that a special blessing must have been bestowed upon her at some point in her life—happiness like this was uncommon. As if sensing her thoughts, Edward reached down and gently kissed her forehead, eyes and worked his way down to her petal-soft lips.

"What are you thinking about?" he asked. Mia stared up into her husband's handsome, chocolate features, a twinkle dancing in her gray eyes.

"Oh, I was just thinking of how lucky *I* am."

"Really? What brought all this on?" Edward asked in mock disbelief.

"What do you mean? I have a handsome husband that I adore and who adores me, a job I love, a beautiful home and last but not least, my health."

"Wow, I guess you're right. You do have a handsome husband," Edward joked.

"Well, Mr. Simone of course," Mia retorted as she raised her head and tickled Edward's side. Edward laughed and the deep timbre of his sexy, baritone voice bounced off the walls and filled the air like music. He pulled Mia closer to him, planting more kisses on her forehead and the bridge of her delicate, freckled nose. Mia pulled the hand-knitted throw over their shoulders and gently rubbed her fingers through the soft hairs on Edward's chest.

"Seriously. I am the lucky one. I have no idea what I would do without you."

"And hopefully you will never have to find out," Mia mused.

"That's right, especially if I have any say in the matter. But, as I said before, I'm very proud of you. My wife, the author. I feel like I'm married to a famous person. Hmmm," Edward said thoughtfully as he rubbed his goatee.

"I feel like Steadman and that would make you Oprah."

"That's funny, I don't feel like a millionaire."

"Well, that's just a matter of time. You have a gift Mia. You've found your niche in life and sometimes it takes people a lifetime to do that, if they find it at all."

"I suppose you're right. It's just that I guess I get scared sometimes. It seems like when things are going too good for people something really bad is thrown at them to..." Mia's voice trailed off.

"To what Mia?" Edward asked as mild concern furrowed his brow.

"I don't know. I suppose I'm getting weird. I was going to say— to even things out. That's just always how it has appeared to me. The scary part is that you don't know how bad the bad is going to be."

"Mia, you're being superstitious. For some, things go from good to better. You have to take these things in stride and be optimistic. The glass is always half full."

"I knew I married you for a reason. You're so rational and clear-headed," Mia chided, lightening the mood.

"Well, that's how we CFO's think—rationally. So, tell me, how is the new book coming along?"

"It's coming along slowly. It's kind of tricky writing a sequel, keeping all the facts straight and consistent with the details of the original story."

"I imagine too, that you must be hard pressed to recall all your character's psychological profiles as well."

"That's true, but thankfully, Dr. Barbara Fischer has agreed to meet with me again so that I can gain more insight on my characters. It really helps me to relate to the villain in the story. And, I owe it to my fans to write this sequel. It seems that every hit on my web-site asks me what happened to Valerie? Did she die?"

"Did she?"

"Well, I kind of left it open to the imagination.

Depending on how you perceived the book, you could think she died or lived, however miserably."

"Yeah, I didn't perceive from it that she died. How far along are you with the sequel?"

"I'm approximately ten chapters into it, but after I meet with Dr. Fischer tomorrow, that may change. I'll either have to do a re-write of what I already have or the good doctor will give me everything I need to plow forward."

"Well, it sounds like you have a good lead on the story. What time are you scheduled to meet with Dr. Fischer tomorrow?"

"My appointment is for 9:00 a.m., but I need to drop my car off at the shop for a tune-up, so I was just going to hop a cab to Dr. Fischer's office."

"That's not necessary, I'll just go in to the office a little late and drop you off at Dr. Fischer's."

"That's sweet, but you don't have to. I don't want to interfere with your schedule."

"Forget about it. It's done. Plus, whenever we can spend some extra time together, we should do it."

"Tell me again, how did I get so lucky?"

"Believe me, I'm the lucky one. I don't know what my life would be like without you, babe."

As Mia stared around the living room at the empty Chinese food containers and clothes strewn everywhere, she responded, "Well, one thing is for sure, your life would definitely be a lot neater." They laughed in unison and were quiet for several moments. But theirs was a comfortable, companionable silence. Mia stared thoughtfully into the yellow-orange fire as Edward gently smoothed her long, wavy, brown, hair.

"What are you thinking about now?" Edward asked.

A silly grin appeared on Mia's face, "Oh, just that one of these days we'll have to see if we can make it upstairs to our bedroom to make love." They both laughed contentedly as the fire crackled noisily above the soft music.

The morning was slightly cool, but Mia still opted to wear her mint colored, linen pantsuit. As was typical of Los Angeles weather during the summer months, though cool now, it would be warm and muggy by noon. Wilshire Boulevard would soon become a sea of convertibles, halter-tops and shorts. Mia inhaled what some believed was fresh, crisp air, into her lungs. If she did not have to meet with Dr. Fischer and run other errands, she too would join the ranks of Angelinos in their materialistic bliss.

Mia crossed the busy intersection onto Wilshire, ignoring the honking horns, wolf whistles and catcalls as she passed three city workers repairing a pothole in the street. She had insisted that Edward let her out across the street so that he wouldn't have to go out of his way to get on Interstate 405 to his office in Santa Monica. Mia entered the three-story building filled with prominent psychologists, counselors and other specialists.

Upon entering the sparsely furnished lobby, she marveled at the huge color television that stood in the corner of the mezzanine waiting area. She chuckled to herself as the waiting patients glued themselves to the large television screen. As she waited for the elevator, she heard the announcer reveal the story for the day, *Women Who Sleep With Their Son's Best Friends*.

Mia entered the elevator and rode up to the third floor. She exited to an empty reception area. Moments later, a young, Asian girl with the silkiest black hair Mia had ever seen, rushed behind the large oak desk. She apologized for her absence and then asked Mia's name and whom she was there to see.

"I'm Mia Simone and I'm here to see Dr. Fischer," Mia replied smoothly. She noticed the girl's beautiful, slanted eyes widen as if she had just discovered something.

"Are you Mia Simone the author who wrote *A State of Mind*?"

"I certainly am."

"Wow!" the receptionist exclaimed. "I am more than halfway through the book now and can hardly wait to see what happens."

"Well, what do you think so far?"

"I'm really enjoying it. I can hardly put it down. I try and read it at my desk, whenever I have a chance. But, 'ya know." The young girl looked around as if to say, 'I can't read here very much.' I'm usually a slow reader. I just bought the book three days ago and I'm almost done."

"Well I'm glad to hear it. That's the most rewarding thing for me to hear as a writer."

"Can you please autograph my book? I have it right here in my bag."

"Sure."

The girl looked away embarrassed and then said, "Oh, Ms. Simone I'm so sorry for wasting your time like this. Let me buzz Dr. Fischer and let her know you're here."

"Don't mention it. It's really not a bother. What's your name?"

"Elizabeth, but please address it to Liz."

Mia signed the book and returned it to the young girl. Within seconds Dr. Fischer appeared at the door which led to the doctors private offices. Dr. Fischer was the most stylish doctor Mia had ever seen. Her warm, brown eyes, smooth skin and hip sense of humor could be deceiving, but the prominent gray hairs along her hairline in her otherwise dark-brown hair, revealed that she must be in her mid-forties. She was about 5'5, with a svelte figure, that was complemented by her beige, silk blouse and long, snug-fitting camel skirt.

"Dr. Fischer, thank you for squeezing me into your busy schedule. I really appreciate it."

"Oh, don't mention it. And call me Barbara, Mia. I think we know each other well enough to be on a first-name basis. Anyway, only my patients call me Dr. Fischer."

"Okay, Barbara," Mia said smiling.

"Right this way."

Mia followed Dr. Fischer down a long corridor and into a large corner office richly furnished with a matching Mahogany desk and credenza. A burgundy, leather chaise typically seen in psychiatrist's offices sat adjacent to the window, overlooking a beautiful view of Rodeo Drive. The office was bright and airy despite the dark-colored ensembles. The colorful floral arrangement complemented by an expensive Tiffany vase added the splash of color the comfortable office required.

"I'm always so taken by this view, Barbara. I don't know how you get any work done."

"I don't, I just let my patients drone on while I pretend to take notes, but I actually just stare into the window of Saks to see what I can buy on my lunch hour," Dr. Fischer joked as she walked over to the window where Mia stood.

Both women shared a laugh like women often do when they know exactly what the other means.

"Yeah, it is pretty amazing. I've actually sat here and seen people arrested right in front of Herme's for shoplifting. It can be a pretty distracting view."

"I'll bet."

"Well, I hope you received my thank you note for listing me in your acknowledgments of *A State of Mind*." By the way, I hear it's a great book."

"Thank you, I couldn't have done it without your help. I can't tell you how much it means to me. Now, I won't take up much of your time because I can still use most of my notes from our last visit."

Dr. Fischer took her seat behind the desk and Mia sat at one of the two chairs opposite her.

"Okay, shoot. What do you need to know?"

"Well, I'm writing a sequel to my last book. As you know, you gave me the psychological profile for a pedophile, which would apply to a kidnapper, rapist, murderer, sadist, etc."

"Right," Dr. Fischer concurred.

"Well, my villain was a kidnapper who possessed these feelings of inadequacy due to being mistreated as a teenager. He had been spurned in his youth, shunned and ridiculed for being 'different' because he had been caught in high school spying on girls in their locker room. On another occasion, he was caught masturbating in the group home in which he lived. And then, he himself was sexually abused as a child. Now, we know that all these things more often than not will cause a child to have emotional problems well into their adult life, but what would cause a person like this to begin kidnapping people?"

"Wow, you sound like the doctor now," Dr. Fischer joked.

"Learned from the best. But, what I want to know in layman's terms is what would provoke a person like this to begin acting violently all of a sudden—to actually begin forcing his behavior on others. So far with the things that I've named, he hasn't hurt anyone really but himself, right?"

Dr. Fischer pulled her long hair into a bun and secured it with a pencil as she glanced thoughtfully out the window. "Well, there are a number of things that could provoke even a stable person to begin to act violently or differently. However, for someone like this it could be that they are suffering from the opposite of spontaneous remission, which is the disappearance of symptoms without formal treatment. Also, there is dementia, which is a form of psychosis or insanity where there is a great impairment of the intellect, memory and other personality traits. Then, there is functional psychosis, which is a severe mental disorder derived primarily from psychological stress and with no apparent organic origin. The probability of hypermania, a kind of manic behavior is characterized by unfriendliness, hostility and aggression. Now, a lot of people with these symptoms blend right in to everyday life and mingle with people like you and me. But, something as simple as a breakup with a girlfriend or boyfriend or the loss of a loved one or even their job could provoke a significant difference in their behavior. So, you can basically take your pick of the psychopathic deviate your character will portray."

"Wow! I wasn't expecting to have so much to choose from," Mia stated as she flicked the off switch on her recorder.

"There's a host of other disorders that I could list for you if you'd like, such as obsessives who pursue in predictable patterns with unwanted phone calls, flowers, etc. Often times rejection triggers the obsession. They feel totally out of control. Sometimes obsessives give up, sometimes they go to someone else and sometimes...." Dr. Fischer hesitated for a moment searching for the right words. "They become dangerous," she continued. "The goal of the obsession often changes. Instead of the object of his obsession being the person who has brought him so much joy, this person now causes him great pain and the obsessor will now be out for revenge."

Mia swallowed hard, "I think I'm okay. That was exactly what I needed—to find out the history of this type of person, his personality and other possible traits and then what would make them assume one bad trait but then escalate to something else. You've given me great insight and a lot to go on. Thank you."

"Well, I'm glad I could be of help. Also, I have to tell you, business has picked up significantly since your book. I have a lot of patients who have read your book and just by your listing my name in your acknowledgments, they have chosen to come here, so I have to thank you for that."

"I'm glad I could help. But, I have to ask you, have you read the book yet?"

Dr. Fischer looked embarrassed, "Well, I'm ashamed to say that I really haven't read past the first three chapters. But my receptionist fills me in on every chapter she reads. I'm really bad about recreational reading. I have so many trade journals that it's unbelievable."

"Believe me, I understand. Anytime you're in a public profession, the world writes you."

"I'm glad you understand, but I'm embarrassed and it's really no excuse. I do plan to start where I left off this weekend."

"Well, I'm not upset. I realize what a busy schedule you have and thank you again for seeing me and giving me your professional opinion."

"You're very welcome, Mia." Both ladies shook hands warmly. Mia gathered her belongings and Dr. Fischer walked her to the reception area.

"Good luck with the book. And, let me know if you need anything else."

"I will, Barbara and thanks again...for everything."

Mia stepped out into the bright May sun. In the hour she had been in Dr. Fischer's office, it had become considerably warmer. She had another hour remaining before her car would be ready. *Maybe I'll do some shopping*, she thought. Mia sauntered in and out of several shops along Rodeo Drive enjoying the freedom that her writing career had afforded her. She still had to stop by the library, the post office and the cleaners before she went home and started work. With her packages in tow, Mia slipped into the nearest Starbucks and relaxed over a scone and latte'. She perused the latest issue of FIT and remembered that she had not had her morning workout and definitely shouldn't be eating the scone. She pushed the half-eaten scone aside and gathered her belongings. Enjoying the warm weather, she pushed her sunglasses up on the bridge of her freckled nose and walked a block to the nearest hotel to hail a cab.

"Where to Miss?" the cab driver asked.

"The main library," Mia replied.

The taxi pulled away from the curb and into the slow moving traffic. Mia tossed her bags aside and referred to her itinerary for her next book signing in San Francisco.

Chapter Three

The cabin area of the old van steamed in the eighty-degree heat. The air conditioning breathed its last more than eight summers ago and duct tape completely covered the broken passenger side window. Discarded food wrappers littered the floor of the van front to back. As Parker McKinley sat waiting for the woman to come out of the medical building, he chewed methodically on a candy bar. Chocolate smeared his lips and teeth and peanut crumbs fell freely into his unkempt beard. Parker didn't care. He was a free spirit who lived out of his van when he wasn't at his trailer park home in a remote area near the Santa Monica Mountains. He had purchased a second-hand motorhome six years ago and found a semi-community primarily to receive his mail and more specifically, his State disability checks. The remote location of the park was ideal for those who did not blend into society so easily. Receiving these checks reminded him of winning the lottery, for the steady money afforded him the opportunity to do whatever he wanted. He had always considered himself a loner and a wanderer. Until he read this book, he liked things the way they were because he didn't have to trust anyone but himself and he knew that he wasn't going to let himself down. The five years he spent locked in a storm shelter in Arkansas as a child had proved to him that he was the only person he could trust. Even the rats and insects he played with and tortured eventually died. Whether it was by natural causes or because he came up with new and creative ways to inflict pain upon them, the fact still remained that no one could be there for him like he could.

These days there wasn't one single thing that he cared about except a particular lovely, young woman. He often fantasized about her, wondering what it would be like the first time he touched her silky, soft skin or smelled her breath. He bet it smelled like sweet caramel or maybe it was the candy bar he was currently devouring. Parker shivered at the thought, but he couldn't be bothered with such idleness at this moment. Knowing where she lived helped him to put thoughts like that out of his head because he knew that he could really be with her any time he wanted. Having so much free time had also enabled Parker to keep track of Mia over the past six months. However, finding out where she lived had proved even easier. He had simply followed her and her loser husband after a local book signing. *Anyone with any sense would have known that they were being followed*, Parker thought angrily. He knew that Edward Simone could never take care of Mia the way she should be taken care of. Her book had proved that. The character, Benjamin Dodds, was more like Parker than a twin could have ever been. When he read the book, he felt like he was reading a chapter of his own life...watching it unfold before his very eyes. Everything about Benjamin Dodds leapt off the page at him and it was then that Parker knew he had to rescue Mia. But he couldn't focus on that right now. Right now, he had to make sure that he didn't lose track of the beautiful, talented, young lady, who had written such an exciting story about them.

When she came out of the medical building, she stood for a moment as if unsure of which direction to go. She was so smart and beautiful and cared enough about him to write a book in his honor. She really had no idea that the character she had created was already alive and living in LA. Parker couldn't wait to put his plan into action, but for now, his job was to sit back and observe.

Chapter Four

Mia stared blankly at the screen trying to work through the writer's block that had been clouding her thoughts for almost an hour now. She swiveled in her silver, mesh, ergonomically correct chair as if she were a kid in a furniture store. She tapped her fingers rhythmically against the desk and turned the radio up slightly when she heard her favorite song playing. She looked at her watch, surprised that it was almost lunchtime already. Giving way to her writer's block, she entered the kitchen through the sunken family room that was adjacent to the home office and filled the teakettle with water. She had made tuna salad last night and removed it from the refrigerator so that it would become room temperature. As she removed an orange-pekoe tea bag from the tin box, the telephone rang, startling her. She was glad for the distraction and quickly picked up the wall phone in the kitchen. She knew from the background noise that it was her friend, Lynda, calling from her cellular phone.

"Mia, can you hear me?" Lynda yelled into the receiver.

"Not clearly. Where are you? You're in a bad transmitting area, I can hardly understand you."

There was a brief pause, silence as if the phone had gone dead and then, Lynda came through clearly.

"Okay. Sorry, I was going under a tunnel."

"Why aren't you at the bookstore?"

"Well, you know that's the beauty of being the boss. The bookstore will survive while I'm away for a few hours. Plus, my assistant Gerry is more than capable of handling things while I'm out and he has my cell phone number should he ever have the need to reach me. However, like I said, he's more than capable. But, I was calling to see if you wanted to do Tae-Bo today."

"What are you up to, Lynda? You know I've got all three videos right here."

"I know, I know. But there's nothing like LA and having Billy Blanks instruct you in person."

"Okay, count me in."

"Wow, that was much easier than I thought. I was all prepared to give you twenty-five reasons why you should take a break and come with me. But I guess I can save them for next time."

"You certainly can, seeing as how you're not taking me away from anything productive. I've had writer's block for the past hour. I honestly don't think I've typed more than a page so far today and that came from the notes of the meeting I had yesterday with Dr. Fischer."

"Well, maybe this is just what you need to clear your head. The class doesn't start until 2:00 o'clock. Have you had lunch yet?"

"I was just about to. Do you want to do lunch here?"

"That would be great. I'm going to swing by the post-office and should be there in about half an hour."

"Great. See you then."

Mia hung up the phone glad to take her mind off writing for a little while. She had no idea that writing a sequel would prove to be so difficult. Seems no matter what you do in life, topping success is hard. She knew that this was part of her writer's block...the fear of this book not being as good or as well received as her first. She placed the phone back on the wall mount and was startled by the whistling of the teapot. While pouring the steaming, hot water over the tea bag, she decided to change into her workout gear while it cooled. Upstairs in her bedroom, Mia pulled on a gray, cotton, two-piece, halter with leggings that accentuated her already svelte figure. She pulled her long, naturally wavy hair back into a ponytail with a matching scunci and took a final look in the full-length mirror that covered the closet door. Satisfied with her appearance and feeling more upbeat now and with the pressure of writing somewhere in the distance, she picked up her cup of tea and sipped gingerly. In *A State of Mind*, the plot focused on the two main characters—the writer and a deranged recluse who lived in a trailer park just outside of Las Vegas. The nightmare begins for the writer when she is abducted on her way home from the grocery store and taken to her kidnapper's hideaway. There, she is held captive by a person who had read her book and begins to play out its scenes in vivid detail. She learns that the only way for her to stay alive is to get inside the mind of her kidnapper and play along. She dares to call him a fan, as he is just a lunatic who proved himself as incapable of separating the truth from reality.

People had been so shocked at the fact that the book had ended with Valerie no longer trying to escape at every turn, but rather choosing to live out her life with her abductor. Benjamin had convinced Valerie that if she ever left him, he would get her back— even if that meant killing anyone he had to in the process. Though it didn't seem like it, the book probably didn't have what most people considered a happy ending—but Valerie survived. Which was the premise of the book. But is surviving enough? Mia knew people would wonder and left the ending deliberately so it could be taken up in the next book.

Mia scrolled back to the first chapter of, *A State of Affairs*, the sequel to *A State of Mind*. She had allowed her character, Valerie Lassiter, to endure eighteen months of terror, psychotic outbursts and cigarette burns at the hands of a mad man. Mia began to read through the pages on the screen: *Valerie had seen the sun only once since she had been kidnapped. Once she had almost reached freedom after spending what must have been days cutting the duct tape that bound her hands together. The sharp piece of metal that stuck out from under the makeshift couch-bed in the filthy trailer had proved almost as effective as a knife. Once her hands were free, she tore off the cloth that covered her eyes. With her right eye peeking between the gritty slats of blinds she saw what must be sunset. But, before she could discern where she was she was slammed, back first on the floor, pain searing through her like a raging fire. He roughly jerked her head up and bound her eyes again before she could even choke on the ever-present gag in her mouth. She could feel the bile rise in her throat and the coppery taste of blood. Her head swam and she did battle with her body to keep her mind conscious.*

"You don't want to upset me," she could hear in the distance, but knew from the hot, stale air and moisture that her abductor must be directly in front of her.

"I'm not gonna let you ruin this for us, Val. Do you hear me?"

She could barely nod her head for the pain that seemed to engulf her...

Mia reread through her first chapter. She should probably be seeing Dr. Fischer professionally for thinking of a storyline as sordid as this and allowing someone — even a fictional character— to endure such hardship.

The doorbell rang and Mia almost jumped out of her chair, spilling most of the hot tea onto her leggings. "Ouch!—This workout is just what I need," she mumbled to herself as she trotted through the living room to answer the door.

"Hey— What happened?" Lynda asked as her attention was immediately drawn to the large, wet, stain on Mia's leggings.

"Oh nothing, I'm just being a klutz today is all," Mia said, irritated, as she patted the stain with one hand and held the dripping teacup in the other.

"Well, I'll prepare the lunch and you get changed. That'll save us some time. I didn't think it would take me so long to get here, but there was a four-car collision on Ventura. It was almost impassable, I thought, 'Oh no! We're going to miss Billy Blanks in one of those tight, little Speedo outfits he's so famous for."

"You're crazy," Mia said laughing with her friend. She was especially glad for her company today. The fact that she had stared at the screen for longer than twenty minutes, was a good indication that she was not going to be very productive today. She couldn't put her finger on it, but she had been feeling ill at ease lately. The fact that she had attended two more author events without seeing her usual visitor had not settled her nerves any, but she refused to reveal her concerns to Edward until she was absolutely sure. Since she hadn't noticed him at the past couple events, she could only assume that the work she was doing on her current book had her spooked. She would work out today and try to put the entire incident behind her. "And we wouldn't want to keep Mr. Blanks waiting now would we? You know, I'm glad you called—I really needed a change of pace from staring at the computer screen."

"That's what I'm here for. I know you'll stay in front of that computer until your eyes cross up."

"I'm not that bad."

"I don't know about that."

"Well, I never —" Mia feigned insult. "Girl, the tuna salad is on the counter and the soup is warming on the stove."

###

Mia sat with her eyes closed on the porcelain bench inside the steam room, thoroughly enjoying the feel of the steam relaxing her taut body. She worked out at home, but Lynda was right when she said there was nothing like doing it in person. Although Billy Blanks was nice to look at, she had the real 'Mr. Universe' at home, she thought wickedly. She really felt good and her mind seemed clear of the fog she had experienced earlier. Mia looked over at a silent Lynda and the five other women in the steam room with them. Normally, one would expect the steady hum of chatter that magically happens when women get together, but there was a peace here and Mia decided to partake in the appreciated quietude.

As Lynda expertly maneuvered her black Landcruiser through the huddle of traffic on Van Nuys

Boulevard, Mia closed her eyes and sank further into the plush leather seats, enjoying the soft music wafting from the CD player. Mia couldn't remember the last time she felt so relaxed.

"Wasn't that great?" Lynda asked breaking Mia's reverie.

"It certainly was. I'm going to have to let you talk me into doing that more often. It makes me never want to use the videotape again," Mia said without ever opening her eyes.

"Believe me I know the feeling. I never envisioned myself taking Tae Kwon Do or anything similar to it and liking it so much. It's absolutely amazing," Lynda said as she shook her head in disbelief. "I also never thought I would find a man who would make me even think about settling down until...Michael, that is." Lynda glanced out of the corner of her eye waiting for her friend's reaction.

"Excuse me! Who is Michael?" Mia yelped, sitting up and repositioning herself in the seat. "And just how long have you been holding out on me?" Mia asked. Smiling smugly, Lynda responded, "I knew that would get your attention. Boy, I wish I had my camera now." Mia folded her arms under her breasts and made an impatient smack of her lips, "I'm serious Lyn. How long has this been going on?"

"Okay, okay," Lynda said as she regained her composure and dabbed at the tears in her eyes. "His name is Michael Bledsoe and you haven't missed a thing, it's only been a week and a half."

"But I just talked to you two days ago and you didn't say a word," Mia interrupted.

"That's because you would have blown it all out of proportion just like you're doing now. Like I was saying before I was so rudely interrupted. It's been a week and a half and I met him in my bookstore. He came in looking for a cook book."

"Hmmm. Sounds suspicious to me," Mia replied. "I mean what was the occasion? Who was he trying to impress?"

"Look Columbo, it was a wedding gift. He told me that his best friend had just been married and his wife wasn't exactly 'Yan Can Cook'. We had a really nice conversation about restaurants and we went to dinner last night."

"What?" Mia asked incredulously. "You went out to dinner with him?"

"I sure did. And, I had a good time too. But now that's really all there is to tell. We have a date scheduled for tomorrow and maybe I'll have more to tell you."

"Well, I'm impressed and you know I want to hear everything."

"Believe me I know," Lynda said as she rolled her eyes heavenward.

"What restaurant are you going to?"

"I thought we'd go to my favorite place."

"Wolfgang Pucks," they said in unison.

"That's right," Lynda laughed. "It's not too intimate, yet open and airy. Also, I think it has the right ambiance and of course, they serve really great food."

"Yeah, I guess that's okay."

"Well thank you very much for your approval, mother dear." The two women laughed together as Lynda struggled to keep focused on the road ahead. A quick glance in the rear-view mirror revealed a vehicle approaching a little too fast for Lynda's taste. She quickly changed lanes to let the vehicle pass, dismissing him as another crazy LA driver.

Chapter Five

Mia had worked frantically over the past two months to complete her manuscript by the scheduled deadline. She had done so successfully and was now flying in from the last city on her book tour. At last, with the final bookstore behind her, Mia raced through the terminal at San Francisco International Airport trying to catch her United flight back to LAX, struggling with her briefcase and laptop to reach the boarding gate. She was thankful she'd worn the most comfortable pantsuit she owned with her flat Enzo Angiolini loafers. It provided a sleek, professional look and was perfect for flying because the fabric remained wrinkle-free. She noticed that she was the only person in line as she was greeted by a reservationist who informed her that the United flight scheduled to depart SFO at 8:20 p.m. had been delayed. Its new expected departure time was now 8:45 p.m. Mia checked in and took a seat among the restless, prospective passengers in the waiting area. She called home and after two rings received the answering machine. Instead of leaving a message, she pressed one of the programmed keys on her cellular phone to reach her husband at the office. Edward picked up on the third ring.

"Edward Simone." The deep timbre of his voice spoke authoritatively into the phone.

"Burning the midnight oil, Mr. Simone?"

"Hi baby," Edward's voice immediately softened as he turned his focus from the pile of papers on his desk to the panoramic view of the Santa Monica skyline that lay before him. "Where are you sexy lady?"

"Sitting in SFO. My flight has been delayed by twenty-five minutes, so I should be home around 10:30 p.m."

"Let me guess, fog in San Francisco?"

"Yep. How was the budget meeting?"

"To say it was grueling would be an understatement."

"That bad, huh?"

"Worse. The Board wants to cut our workforce by twenty percent. That means laying off one hundred employees!" Edward said, virtually screaming into the receiver.

"Ouch! I'm sorry you had such a bad day, honey."

"It's not your fault, baby," he said in a calmer tone. "I just can't wait to see you."

"The feeling is mutual," Mia replied as she observed a thirty-something man construct a makeshift bed on the uncomfortable terminal chairs. It always amazed her at how people could sleep in public like that. But, then again, sleep was very powerful. If people could fall asleep at the wheel of a car, they could fall asleep anywhere.

"What's your flight number? I'll pick you up from the airport."

"No, no. I drove and parked, thinking I'd be home by 9:30 p.m. or so, but anyway, I don't want to inconvenience you."

"Mia, please stop it. It's not an inconvenience. Plus, it's going to be late."

"No, sweetie. I'll be fine. Anyway, I want to sleep in tomorrow and I don't want to have to get up early to pick my car up from the airport."

With great resignation, Edward agreed, "Okay, but you call me at home if you're too tired or anything. And, call me anyway at home as soon as you land. I'm leaving here in about half an hour."

"You know, you worry too much," Mia teased. "But, I'll call, okay? Oh, and my flight number is 1255."

"Okay," Edward agreed, his voice dropping an octave as he scribbled down the flight number, "And if you're not too tired, maybe I can give you a back rub."

"My, my Mr. Simone, that statement was just filled with innuendo," Mia replied. She twirled a lock of hair around her finger as she thought about the last time they were together.

"Yes, it certainly was and I meant every word. I'll try to wait up for you."

"You do that."

"I love you."

"I love you, too."

Mia settled back to wait. Her agent had called last week and informed her of a change in her book tour schedule. She would need to go to San Francisco in three days, rather than in two weeks. That left Mia with two days instead of eight to pack. But it would conclude her tour more quickly. Edward had accompanied her to Baltimore and Atlanta as he had managed to do for every city she had visited on her tour so far. But, his firm had an all-day budget meeting today that required his attendance and Mia had been on her own in "Frisco" as she had heard it affectionately termed so many times throughout the day. Her book signings at two prominent bookstores had gone very well. The audience was supportive, receptive, refreshingly vocal and best of all; this audience really wanted to know when her next book was coming out. She was careful not to mention that her next book was a sequel, but did assure them that she was working on something that she was excited about and would try not to disappoint them. She was sure too, that her lighthearted mood was also attributed to the fact that she hadn't spied her fan in the audience. *Maybe it was just a phase*, she thought.

After signing more than one hundred books and copies for the stores, her hand and forearm ached. She was always surprised to see how many people read her books. But more surprising was how much her fans cared about the characters in the book. It was almost as if they didn't realize that the people in the book *were* made up characters. Mia would never forget when she and Edward were out grocery shopping one evening a month after *A State of Mind* was in stores. An elderly lady walked up to her in the produce section of the store, pointing a wrinkled, accusatory finger.

"How could you let such a thing happen to Valerie?" She hissed. "You ought to be ashamed," she continued. Mia and Edward exchanged looks of disbelief. "I prayed and prayed, but you just would never let her get out of that situation."

Mia was speechless. Before her mind could begin to formulate a response the lady had turned on her heels and was making her way back down the aisle. After the initial shock, Edward laughed, but the oddness of the incident resonated in Mia's mind and hung over her like a dark cloud. It wasn't until later that evening that she decided she *had* to write a sequel to the story. She knew that there was no way to satisfy every reader, but she felt compelled to satisfy at least one—the little old lady in the grocery store.

Mia absently massaged her hands as she often did when in thought. Writing was such a wonderful gift to be able to share. The receptions today had been uplifting and she had come away with a renewed sense of just how fortunate she was. She couldn't wait to get home and tell Edward about her trip and begin to celebrate their seven-year anniversary. She reached down in the little powder blue shopping bag and extracted a matching powder blue jewelry box. The engraved, sterling silver pocket watch she purchased had cost her a pretty penny, but her husband was definitely worth it she thought, as a smile played across her lips. The silver gleamed against the velvety softness of the case. Mia read the inscription: *Happy 7th Anniversary—you complete me.*

Feeling surprisingly relaxed and invigorated, Mia put the watch away, set up shop and cranked away at notes for her book while waiting for her flight to be announced.

###

Parker McKinley sat in the rear of the plane where he could keep his eye on Mia. Fortunately, the plane was empty enough that he could choose the seat he wanted, but crowded enough to shroud him among the other passengers. He had waited so long for this night. In actuality, it had only been six months ago, since her book had come out in reprint again, that he decided he had to be with the beautiful woman that graced the back cover page of the book written for and about him. It had been long enough. He would share her with the rest of her fans for only so long. Now, it was his turn. As the pilot announced their eminent departure, Parker became more excited by the moment. Patience was definitely a good thing and he had most certainly been patient...and it had paid off. He knew that her 'hot shot' husband couldn't possibly attend every signing with her because his job was much too important to him. But, Parker would treat her in a way that she could only come to respect and he would certainly never let her travel alone, if in fact, he ever let her out of his sight long enough to travel at all. However, all these things would come in time. First, he would have to convince Mia Simone that what he had done was best for her and second, he would have to convince her that she loved him as much as he loved her.

"A piece of cake," he spoke aloud.

"Excuse me?" the passenger two seats over asked.

Unaware that he had spoken aloud, Parker looked over at the gentleman staring at him with a bewildered look on his face.

"Did you say something?" the man asked.

"No I did not," Parker hissed, his voice barely a whisper. The glint in his eyes revealing his dementia. Parker could see and smell the fear in the man as he swallowed hard and wiped at his sweaty forehead. After an awkward silence, the man turned his back to Parker and stared out the window.

The plane descended smoothly into LAX and taxied on the runway. When it came to a full stop, the passengers scrambled out of their seats, gathering their belongings from under the seats and the overhead compartments. Parker remained seated, with watchful eyes on Mia. She was so beautiful and innocent, as she would be in the very moment when her life would change forever.

The flight had been quick, smooth and uneventful and Parker had gone undetected by Mia. In fact, she never turned around once during the entire flight, which worked out perfectly for Parker. However, even if she had noticed Parker, dressed in a black baseball cap, dark khakis, a black, short-sleeved tee shirt and black Converse tennis shoes, it would not have made much difference. His appearance was going to take on a dramatic change once he and Mia were together.

Parker kept a safe distance behind Mia as they walked through the terminal. He was glad he had chosen to travel light by not bringing a coat or travel bag. Because the trip to San Francisco had only been a one-day trip, he didn't bring a change of clothing either, but fastened around his ankle was a travel wallet that contained a cotton handkerchief and small bottle of ether. Although he did not anticipate many people in the short-term parking lot at this hour, if he was quick, he would not have to worry about causing a scene.

He chuckled gleefully under his breath. Deliberately he hadn't gone to either of her two book signings while in San Francisco. He didn't want to reveal himself before he put his plan into action. He was pleased with how smart he was. Also, if Mia had become alarmed and noticed him, again, she might have had her husband meet her at the airport, which would have delayed his plan even further. Unwilling to take the risk, he stayed in close proximity of the bookstores she visited, but never went in. Over the past two or three signings Mia hadn't noticed him. He had to be extremely careful now. The first time she really noticed him, she became slightly distracted and stuttered during the reading, but quickly recovered. There was never any doubt in Parker's mind that she would notice him because he knew she didn't have any reader as committed to attending every reading. Now, as he went undetected, trailing Mia through the airport, a shiver ran up his spine at the thought of how close he was to having her...forever.

Mia cursed herself as she walked to the parking garage. *I should have had Edward pick me up*, she thought aloud as she pressed the power button on her cellular phone. In her haste to catch her flight to San Francisco, she had settled for the only available parking spot on the seventh floor of a ten level parking garage and a million miles away from the nearest elevator. As she walked through the predominantly desolate garage, the only sound was her echoed footsteps. She returned the phone to the side compartment of her purse and extracted a small container of pepper spray. Looking around for other people, she spotted a lady about two hundred feet away entering her vehicle. Feeling increasingly uneasy, she clutched her laptop in her left hand and her car keys in her right as she quickened her pace. She approached her car, deactivated the alarm and slid the key into the door's lock. Just as she placed her hand on the handle to open the door, she caught movement out of the corner of her right eye. But, before she could process what she had actually seen, a hand clamped over her mouth. As Mia struggled for control over her breathing and consciousness, her thoughts quickly resorted to the fact that this could not be happening. This was the type of thing people read about. As she tried to remember details for the police, the rapidly encroaching darkness fell upon her like a wet blanket. Total blackness as deep and unending as any ocean lapped and chipped away at the remaining light until she was lost in its abyss.

###

Parker knelt on the passenger side of Mia's black Lexus. After carefully noting where she had parked and her license plate number, his plan to wait for her at the car worked perfectly. Pleasure settled over him almost sinful in nature. He had an entire five minutes to get himself ready and pour the ether onto the cotton cloth. Parker had waited for this moment for what seemed like forever. He would now have someone with him who truly understood and respected how he thought.

He heard her footsteps approaching the car as he sat back on his haunches — ready to spring like a cat. The moment he heard her deactivate the alarm, he knew the countdown had begun. When he was certain that the key had entered the lock, he scurried around to the rear of the car and waited for the perfect moment. He counted to four and made his move, devouring her with the powerful fumes of the ether before she could scream or make a sound. There was very little struggle or resistance. As Mia's body went limp, Parker carefully placed her in the back of the car on the plush leather seats. He popped the trunk and luckily spotted a blanket, which he extracted and placed over Mia's petite frame. He then hurriedly went through her purse and removed a fifty-dollar bill from her wallet along with the parking stub required to exit the garage. Thankful for the slight tint on the windows, Parker expertly maneuvered the Lexus out of the garage and onto the main highway. With the dosage of ether he had given her he knew she would be out for at least two hours. By then, both their lives would have changed in ways they never thought possible.

Chapter Six

12:47 a.m. Edward paced frantically—methodically like a caged panther. Stopping for a brief moment to stare
out the large living room window, as if somewhere in the
darkness the answer to Mia's whereabouts waited his dis-
covery. He hadn't received a call from her as agreed and the
airlines had confirmed flight #1255 arrived at 10:05 p.m.,
over two hours ago. He also confirmed that Mia Simone
was a passenger on the plane.

"Where the hell could she be?" he said aloud, never
missing a beat in his pacing. He snatched up the phone in
the den and punched in the number to Mia's cellular phone
for the eighth time. He received a recorded message each
time indicating that her phone was turned off or she was out
of range. He placed the receiver back in the cradle and shook
his head. A grim picture of Mia lying on the side of the road
flashed in his mind. Running his hands across his hair he
resumed his pacing. Mia was always punctual and when she
couldn't be she made it a habit to at least call. This was
totally unlike her and Edward refused to think that anything
bad had happened. But, the constant wave of nausea in his
belly was calling him a liar.

Grabbing his suit jacket and car keys in one fluid
motion, Edward headed for the front door and out into the
dark night. When he spoke to Mia earlier from his office,
the view provided a starry, beautiful night. Back when they
were dating, Edward and Mia had shared many evenings at
Venice Beach under the same beautiful sky with its starry
backdrop. Now, that same sky appeared dark and ominous
and the once twinkling stars seemed to taunt him. Edward
put his champagne colored Jaguar XJ8 into reverse and sped
off down the quiet, tree-lined street.

###

"Officer Ross," Edward began again. "I under-stand that your policy is that a person has to be missing 24 hours before you can file a missing persons report, but that is very contradicting to the theory that the first eight hours of a disappearance is crucial, and four hours if its a child." His jaw muscle flexed involuntarily as he glowered at the lethargic, overweight officer. He was certain beyond the shadow of a doubt that something had happened to Mia. However, trying to explain the smooth curves of a hyperbo-la would have been easier.

The short, portly officer pursed his thin, pink lips and narrowed his gaze on Edward. "Look Mr. Simone, as you pointed out that is *our* policy. There is nothing we can do right now but take down your information," he pounded a pudgy finger on the worn, wooden desk for emphasis. "And, if we happen across something suspicious then we have your information—" he continued.

"Happen across something?" Edward asked incred-ulously, cutting the officer off mid-sentence. "Happen upon what? My wife's body perhaps. I mean, who the hell do I have to kill here to get the proper attention. I have told you a million times that my wife is missing. She was on her scheduled flight that landed just shortly after 10:00 p.m. She has no family here or within driving distance whose house she would have stopped by at this hour and her only friend in the area, I have already left a message, but I'm sure she's not there." Edward placed his hand over his forehead in exhaustion.

"Ross, I'll handle this. Excuse me ah, mister?" the voice came out of nowhere.

Edward turned to face a tall, dark-skinned, man with the physique of a body builder.

"Simone. Edward Simone." The two men shook hands.

"Sergeant Williams," he said as he patted Edward

on the back and guided him down a corridor and into a small, dank office. As he closed the door behind them, he gestured for Edward to have a seat in one of the two hard, wooden chairs that sat opposite his battered, steel desk. Upon his desk sat stacks of papers, manila file folders and a tiny lamp that provided minimal light. Edward quickly surveyed the dingy walls. His attention was immediately drawn to the to the bulletin board with pictures of at least ten women. As if reading his thoughts, Sergeant Williams said, "All missing." His eyes scanning the unknown faces.

A knot of fear coiled in Edward's stomach, momentarily making him more nauseous than before. He sat down in one of the wooden chairs and faced the sergeant.

"Mr. Simone, I called you in here because I heard bits and pieces of your conversation with Officer Ross and though it breaks our normal protocol," the burly sergeant shook his head and glanced over to the bulletin board filled with faces, "I want to start working on your case right now. As much information as I can get from you would be great. So, by the time twenty-four hours is up, we will have all the information we need to start our full-fledged investigation."

Edward began slowly, methodically, telling the sergeant about his conversation with Mia while she was at the airport. "...And the last thing I said to her was to call me when her flight landed," Edward concluded, his anxiety reaching its boiling point.

Sergeant Williams jotted down thorough notes. When he finished, he looked at Edward and shook his head in exasperation. "Mr. Simone, I can only tell you what you already know, and that is that if our search of the local hospitals don't have any record of admitting your wife, then my best guess is that foul play is involved here. I can certainly believe that if you know your wife and she said she was coming home then that is where she was indeed headed—"

"I don't mean to be rude, Sergeant," Edward interrupted. "But, what do you plan to do to get this investigation underway before twenty-four hours has passed. I want somebody to start doing something now. I have photos, telephone numbers, the make, model and license plate number of her car right here," Edward said pushing a manila envelope across the desk to Sergeant Williams.

"I understand your frustration Mr. Simone. And, I did call you in here for a reason. I am going to do everything I can to help you, because the first hours are critical. I will fill out a report and send two of my men out to the airport to ask some questions."

"Thank you, Sergeant. Thank you. I can't tell you how much this means to me. In the meantime, I'll have fliers printed up and re-trace everything I can think of."

"That sounds fine. Now, you should go home and try to get yourself some rest and be there just in case she calls," Sergeant Williams stated as he began opening the manila envelope.

Standing to leave, Edward turned to the sergeant, "I think you have everything you need including my cell phone number. Please call me if you learn anything of my wife's whereabouts."

Sergeant Williams extracted the pictures and stared blankly, "One thing Mr. Simone, you didn't tell me your wife was a well-known writer."

"I told you that she was a writer and was returning from the last leg of her tour."

"Hmmm," the sergeant fingered his mustache thoughtfully. "This expands the possibilities and really adds to the potential scenarios."

"I really don't like the sound of this, Sergeant," Edward said removing his hand from the doorknob.

"You'll like it even less when you've heard everything. The facts surrounding the disappearances of famous personalities are at best, bizarre. Why don't you have a seat Mr. Simone and tell me, where you were when your wife disappeared?"

He lay across the bed—their bed, barely clothed, thinking of his last conversation with Mia. Weary and grainy-eyed, Edward struggled with thoughts drifting back and forth about the possibilities. What had actually happened seemed like something seen on television, yet it was happening to him. Sergeant Williams' startling revelation about the possibilities of what may have happened to Mia, made Edward physically ill.

Initially, he was insulted at being looked at as a suspect in his wife's disappearance, but quickly learned that Sergeant Williams was just doing his job. Deep down he hoped it would be as simple as someone holding her for ransom, as had been suggested by the sergeant. He was more inclined to believe that it was not random, but rather someone who knew who she was. He just couldn't think of anyone who would want to hurt Mia. But, he *knew* it was not that simple. Yet, the not knowing where or what was happening to his wife was enough to drive him mad. The tension started from the nape of his neck and swiftly reached the bridge of his nose, covering him like a dark cloud. If only he had gone with her, this would never have happened. If it had not been for that damned budget meeting, he would have been there right by her side, allowing no harm to come to her. For the first time since Edward was a young teenager, crying because he didn't win the championship trophy for the All-City basketball team, he cried. Clutching the paisley print comforter, his walnut-colored hands balled into tight fists, Edward cried. He buried his face in Mia's pillow and inhaled the fresh freesia scent from the body oil she wore. The hurt and helplessness ran so deep that he felt his heart would break in two.

As surely as if the photo had beckoned him, Edward's attention was drawn to the picture of he and Mia on the nightstand. It was a picture of the two of them in

Maui. Mia wore a white orchid in her hair—frizzy from the moist, hot climate and warm, tropical breezes. Her smooth skin glistened, adding a delicious honey glow to her complexion, which was beautifully enhanced by the revealing bathing suit she wore. She draped herself seductively over Edward's shoulders with her fingers splayed across his bare, muscular chest. The sheepish grin on his face as bright as the Hawaiian shirt that hung around his biceps. The sugar white sand, turquoise blue ocean and tropical breezes ensured that they would never forget the sun-filled days and steamy nights of their romantic trip to Maui. Edward retrieved the picture and traced the outline of Mia's face with the tip of his finger. He seemed to gain strength just by looking at her "Where are you, baby?" he asked the picture as if it could answer, "Where are you?"

He looked at his watch. It was 6:17 a.m. He had been at the police station for over five hours and had got very little accomplished. As he stripped out of his suit from the day before, he thought about what he would do today. First on his list would be to have fliers printed and pasted on every telephone pole, grocery store window and train station from LAX to the tri-state area. He would then ask his own questions at the airport and garage where she parked her car. He would follow the route that she most likely took from the airport to see if maybe there had been any accidents on the road. And then, he would check with friends and acquaintances to see if they had possibly heard anything. There was no way he was going to sit around for twenty-four hours, until 10:00 p.m. tonight and wait for the police to do something.

Clad in only his boxer shorts, Edward began a rapid succession of push-ups and sit-ups until he lost count. The ringing of the phone brought him out of the exercise haze he was in. With cat-like quickness he got to his feet and snatched up the phone, his breathing ragged and heavy from his calisthenics.

"Hello," he breathed into the phone, struggling to catch his breath.

"Edward," the voice on the other end answered, matching his with its intensity. "Oh my God. I got your message saying that Mia hadn't arrived at home. Tell me she made it home okay." Edward's hesitation immediately clued Lynda in to the fact that Mia had not come home. "She's not there is she?" Lynda asked understanding the reality.

"No Lynda. She's not."

Chapter 7

Mia's head swam as the effects of the ether slowly relinquished its hold. She immediately realized that her hands and feet were bound behind her and that the flat loafers she had on before were no longer on her feet. Totally disoriented, she relied on the senses of smelling and hearing, hoping that something might become familiar —nothing did. The smell was damp and musty which could have meant nothing more than it had rained, but as she struggled to listen, there was only silence. Her first thoughts were of Edward and that she was supposed to call him. Would she ever see him again? Smell the scent of him again? Make love to him again? Her situation seemed dire and the reality was that these were questions she neither had the answers to or any control over. Mia was suddenly bombarded with a thought that chilled her to the core. She knew instinctively what was happening to her as the images of scenes she had read and re-read many times from her very own book, came to life in her mind. A trickle of sweat trailed the length of her neck and traveled between her breasts, coming to rest in her already damp bra. Her covered eyes revealed a deep darkness that prohibited her from knowing whether it was day or night. Mia struggled and kicked, but to no avail. She could ascertain that the area in which she sat was not carpeted, but slippery, like tiles. Her right hip began to throb from the awkward position she was placed in. She could neither sit straight up or lay down, but regardless of her struggles, remained in a quasi-hunched over position. Whenever she tried to stand, her stockinged feet would only slide from beneath her when put up against the tension of the rope and she would come down hard on her rear. She did notice that her shifting seemed to be answered by a gentle swaying, as if on a boat or something without a stable foundation. If only she could see where she was and get her bearings, maybe she could get away. As her fear and anxiety heightened, Mia's breathing came in quick, rapid successions. The room began to spin wildly and just when she thought she would pass out, racking sobs pierced the preternatural silence as the reality of how uncertain her future was, came in vivid imagery.

Mia doubled over in physical and mental anguish. She felt less than human. Tied, bound and without the use of her sight, she would have to rely heavily on her survival instincts. But first, she had to try and regain some semblance of control. The tears stopped flowing, her heartbeat returned to a more normal pattern and the muscles in her cramping abdomen began to relax. She sat up on her haunches and cocked her head slightly to the right, listening for sound. There was none that became immediately discernible. Squeezing her eyes shut under the restricting bound to focus more clearly, she gradually became aware of the faint smell of mold, underlying fumes of gasoline and the sounds of chirping birds. Slowly, she began feeling around the area behind her, where her hands remained tied. The cool, smooth area initially revealed nothing. However, as she inched her way vertically up the side of the wall, she discovered that there was a handle on the surface. It would appear to be a cabinet. Was she in a kitchen or bathroom? Her mind raced with the possibilities of where she could be and who would do something like this. She strained her eyes once again to see against the fabric that covered them and was able to make out images shrouded in shadows. She could discern a small circular table attached to a single cylindrical leg and a U-shaped seating area around it. She was situated in an area immediately adjacent to it. There was a bed that folded out from the wall across from her and above it a small window. To the right, near the U-shaped seating area, but only about a foot away, was an alcove, which Mia assumed was a restroom, however, it was too dark to be sure. She then turned her head to the left and could make out a larger circular table and beyond that, what appeared to be more windows. A chill snaked through her at the thought of being in such close proximity with some-one who had resorted to tying her up and abducting her. She envisioned some heinous, dirty, escaped convict. What would happen to her? Would she be raped or killed? As her adrenaline soared, her heart beat deafeningly in her ears and the thick vein in her neck pulsed to the same macabre rhythm. Just as the fear began to envelop her again, she heard a sound and her breath caught in her throat. It was dif-ferent from the sounds of birds that she'd heard earlier. It was the sound of a door opening and then being pulled shut. There was a cool current of air and then complete silence once again. After a considerable amount of time had passed, Mia almost thought she was alone again, until she heard a voice.

"My beautiful, Mia. I see that you are awake."

Mia's body stiffened at the voice. Not because there was anything significant in it's tone or timbre, but because of the familiarity with which he spoke her name.

She tried to manage words, but the gag in her mouth prevented her, causing bile to rise in her throat as she coughed violently. Parker rushed to her and removed the gag. She felt a clammy hand stroke her cheek and she flinched as though she'd been slapped. A scream caught in her throat, but was silenced by the stern and disturbing pitch in her captor's voice.

"Now Mia, please don't scream or else I will have to replace the gag and make it tighter. I want you to feel comfortable with me and I know that people do that by talk-ing—'ya know telling each other about events that have hap-pened in the other's life. So, I'll go first. When I was grow-ing up, I never had a normal childhood. Whatever memories I had of my biological father were erased by the horrible ones created by my stepfather and loving mother. 'You're a worthless little shit—just like your father,' she'd tell me, he said without rancor. "Her words haunt me even twenty years after her death," he continued. "I actually believed everything she told me. Every put down, every promise, when she was sober, that things were going to be better. I was only ten. She was my mother and I trusted her even when she allowed my stepfather to lock me in the basement for weeks at a time."

Parker stood and paced the tiny vestibule of the trailer. "There was no place to use the bathroom," he laughed to himself. "But, I was going to learn to become a man if it killed me. I even believed her when she told me that we would leave before he killed us both. And when she was killed, it was just another promise that had gone unfulfilled. At ten years of age, I became a ward of the state. With no family that I ever knew of except my grandmother who died when I was two, it seemed the bloodline would end with me. From that day forward, I knew I'd never have a normal life with a wife and children. Sure, I was scrawny, pale and my disinterest in sports and morbid fascination in vermin etched that reality in stone. The highlight of my life was when I turned eighteen and grew hair on my face. It was such a monumental event that I decided to never shave."

His scruffy beard had been full, giving him the appearance of a much older man. He absently rubbed his chin where the reddish-brown bush had covered most of his face. He stooped, his lips slightly grazing the side of Mia's right ear. At 5'8 and 140 pounds, Parker was still scrawny compared to most men, but he was strong and agile. His long, reddish-brown hair worn in a single braid and unkempt beard made him look like a peaceful hippie, but the menacing look in his eyes indicated otherwise. As far back as he could remember, he had always been an outcast and a loner. Absolutely no one that he ever encountered understood him the way he knew Mia would.

"But maybe it's time for a change. You know, a new look—a new life." Mia shrieked back like a cornered animal.

"There is really no need to be afraid, Mia. You are home now, where you belong."

"Who are you?" Mia demanded as a cold, deep, fear snaked throughout her, touching her soul.

"Oh, you'll find that out soon enough."

"What?" Mia asked in horror.

"We definitely know each other," Parker said calmly.

"I don't know you," Mia hissed, her voice laced with contempt. "You're crazy," she continued.

"That's not true, Mia. But, that's not what we're going to talk about right now. I have waited far too long for this moment — the moment when we would be together."

"Please, just let me go," Mia pleaded.

"Now that I have you, Mia, I can never let you go. Can't you understand that? From the moment I first saw you, I knew that we had to be together and I'm really sorry that you don't feel the same way. But, in time, you will feel for me the way I feel for you."

"No," Mia screamed.

"Yes," Parker continued calmly. "Now, there are a few rules that you'll need to abide by in order for us to make this work: Number one; No drinking or smoking, but I'm sure you don't have any of those nasty habits, do you?" he asked not waiting for a response. "Number two; I will feed you until we establish some modicum of trust. At that point, I will release your hands and allow you to feed yourself. And Number three—"

"Fuck you. You filthy son-of-a-bitch."

Parker shook his head in obvious disappointment as he rubbed his chin. He stood over Mia's crouching form and casually reached in the cabinet above the tiny sink and extracted a cigarette lighter and a single cigarette. He flicked the lighter and carefully lit the cigarette, making sure the flames saturated the tobacco to keep it lit. He then took a deep drag of the cigarette, held his breath for a moment and then exhaled.

"You see Mia," he spoke as he took another drag of the cigarette. "I love you and I have never hit a woman before in my life, but I really hate a foul-mouthed person. And so, it is with much regret that I must teach you, like my mother taught me, about swearing." He reached down and grabbed Mia's exposed arm and touched the cigarette to her pale flesh. Mia screamed in agony as the cigarette caused an immediate bubbly, purplish-red circle on her forearm. She sobbed uncontrollably at the thought that her fate was in the hands of a lunatic that she could barely see. What was going to be his next move? Mia craned her head from right to left trying to access the location of her abductor, as the stinging sensation on her arm became a dull throb.

"Now, as I was saying before I was so rudely inter-rupted. Number three; no swearing or screaming. I believe now that we have established the fact that it will not be tol-erated."

Mia composed herself and said with as much con-fidence as she could muster, "I hope you don't think you're going to get away with this. People—the police will come looking for me."

"Don't you think I know that? But of course, by then, we'll be long gone. You see Mia—" Parker crouched, speaking to Mia's blindfolded face. "I've put a lot of thought and time into my plan of our being together and I am not," he slammed his fist down on the cold linoleum floor to drive home his point, "going to let anything prevent that from happening. Not your unlady-like language, not the police and not your hot-shot husband."

Slowly losing her resolve, Mia spoke, "What are you going to do with me?"

"Well, let me put your mind to ease. I'm not going to rape you or kill you. I'm not crazy, Mia. But you will be disciplined if you swear. I just want you to be with me, that's all. I love you and soon you will come to love me too. I just want us to be together."

"Be together? What are you insane?"

"I just told you I'm not," Parker interjected.

"You kidnap me, blindfold me, tie me up and torture me, Mia continued. "And, you call it love. It's just like rape!" Mia said incredulously.

"You don't understand, but in time you will. But enough with the questions right now. It's been almost two days and you need to eat."

"Can you please take off my blindfold?"

"No," Parker said calmly. "Well we'll have to see. No pun intended," he chuckled.

"I need to use the restroom badly," Mia exclaimed, rocking back and forth.

"You know if I were an evil person, I would tell you to just go right where you are —on yourself, like mother used to tell me. But you see this is my first exercise in love. I will allow you go to the bathroom. I will even untie your hands so that you can do what is required. But, I warn you," he kneeled down close to Mia's face and she could smell the sourness of his breath. "Do not betray me. There are two things, in addition to my house rules that I will not tolerate and that is being lied to and being deserted. I'd just as soon kill us both if I had to be without you, Mia. You are the first person who truly understands me."

Mia shook her head as if it would stop the senseless words that this man spoke. What in the world could he be thinking? And, more importantly what did he plan to do with her? That was the most fearful question of all. She had to find a way to get out of here.

Parker slowly untied the secured knot in the rope that bound Mia's arms and led her to the tiny facility that she originally thought was a restroom. She immediately rubbed at the darkening, painful sore on the soft flesh of her left forearm. Once inside the small, dark stall, Mia removed the blindfold from her eyes and frantically searched around the tiny area for something to use as a weapon. Anything she could place in the pocket of her pants or even in her panties and take back out with her. But there was nothing to be found except the small toilet and basin immediately adjacent to it. No mirror or medicine cabinet or anything. Mia sighed in frustration and defeat as she looked down at her still bound ankles.

"Be a good girl and place the blindfold back around your eyes before you come out," Mia heard through the thin door that separated her from the complete stranger on the other side. In total compliance, she conducted her business, careful not to touch the seat, washed her hands and began to place the blindfold back over her eyes. She gave one last cursory glance over the tiny facility to make sure she hadn't missed the opportunity to use anything as a weapon. She hadn't. With that, she turned the knob on the door and shuffled barefoot back out into semi-darkness. Without knowing how long she would be kept blindfolded, maybe she could use the fact that she could see only some images, to her advantage. But, she would have to pretend to be completely blind until the right opportunity presented itself.

"Good girl. Now, while you were in the bathroom, I prepared lunch for us. You have not eaten in two days— you must be starved."

Surprisingly, Mia hadn't thought about how long it had been since she ate, bathed or used the restroom. But, the power of suggestion was amazing. She was suddenly so famished that she felt sick. Whatever this psycho had prepared he must have microwaved if he was able to have it ready that quickly, as she had not smelled or heard anything being prepared prior to her short visit to the restroom. There was a smell of something akin to mashed potatoes and gravy and Mia's stomach growled in anticipation. She was shocked and a little disappointed in herself that she even had an appetite under the circumstances.

Suddenly, a realization much stronger than her hunger dawned on her. Her hands were still free. This was the opportunity she had been looking for and she planned to take full advantage of it.

"You just sit right down here," Parker spoke softly, as if he were tending to the needs of a small child.

Mia knew she had been placed at the circular table that she was able to make out earlier when she took inventory throughout the small camper. A warm meal was soon placed directly in front of her and Mia's stomach responded to the aroma.

"As you can see, I am trusting you. I have not as yet replaced the rope around your wrists. Certainly, I could feed you, but if we are to establish a relationship, there must be trust, don't you agree?"

"Where are my shoes?" Mia demanded, not giving in to his sick line of questioning.

"They're in your car along with that beautiful watch you bought for that man from your past. Humph. I complete you now, Mia."

"And where is my car?" Mia spat sarcastically.

"There will be plenty of time for questions. We have the rest of our lives. Right now, you need to eat."

Parker took Mia's hand and placed her fingers around the fork. He was almost overcome by the softness and beauty of her skin. He had made special preparations for this moment by shaving off his beard. It had been a mask he had hidden behind for many years. First, to celebrate his manhood and then to conceal the shame and disappointment of his childhood. But, this was a time for new beginnings and shaving his beard had been like shedding an old skin. That was one thing that had always fascinated him about snakes, they could always be renewed and forgiven of their past sins by the shedding of their skin.

Being this close to her was something he had dreamt about for months and now it was finally happening.

To have someone be with him and share in his life was something he had never known. Once Mia came to terms with her feelings for him, it would make things that much more wonderful. Parker was certain that subconsciously Mia knew they were meant to be together, she just needed a little time, and he had plenty of it to give.

As Mia felt his sweaty hands envelope hers, she forced back the stinging bile that rose in her throat. When he finally released her hands to feed herself, Mia knew it was now or never.

In one fluid motion, Mia quickly removed the blindfold from her eyes and savagely swung the fork in the direction of Parker McKinley, missing his jugular by a mere fraction of an inch. Before Parker could process what had happened, Mia brought the fork around again, this time creating a hideous gash under his left eye. She then pummeled him with a succession of punches with her left hand while poking and swinging the fork with her right. As Parker ran to grab napkins from the nearby counter, Mia unfastened the knot that bound her ankles and headed for the aluminum door that was no more than four feet away. Parker was coming at her fast, as he held the napkins over his eye, but he tripped before reaching her. Unfamiliar with the door and wasting precious seconds, Mia finally gained access to the outside, but was jerked to a stop by the rope around her neck. Her feet flew out from beneath her as Parker pulled back on the rope. She fought and flailed wildly with every ounce of strength in her. She kicked behind her in roundhouse fashion. She heard and felt herself making contact, but nothing seemed to deter his one-handed grip on the rope. Mia managed to twirl around in the rope feeling it rub roughly against her skin. Mia noticed that her abductor was the same guy that had been at all of her readings, only now, he didn't have a beard. His eyes were unmistakably that of the person at all her book signings. He had purposely changed his appearance.

Mia fought harder as the desperation of her circumstances weighed on her like an anvil. He was not much heavier than she and maybe only a couple inches taller, however, his strength was inhuman. Mia's blows were like feathers landing on a pillow. When her abductor was tired of playing cat and mouse, the last thing Mia remembered was a hard blow to the side of her skull and the all too familiar fall into unconsciousness.

Chapter Eight

"I can't imagine how hard this must be for you, but the best thing you can do right now is go back to work—try to keep your mind busy with other things or else you'll go crazy." Sergeant Williams offered.

"I'm just useless here. I feel like there's something else I could be doing, but I just haven't thought of it yet," Edward said, pressing the receiver to his ear. "And worst of all, no progress is being made. That's what's really killing me."

"Look, Edward, man-to-man, I'm spearheading this case personally and making sure we have our best men on the job. We've canvassed the area here and we're working closely with the chief of police in Los Angeles. Fliers have been made. We've called everyone in Mia's rolodex and fans and associates have set up a command headquarters with volunteers from her book club to answer phones twenty-four hours a day."

"I don't know, man. I just don't know how this could've happened. You always think this type of thing happens to *other* people. And nothing can ever prepare you for it," Edward's voice trailed off.

"Hey look, this case is in excellent hands—mine. Your coming down to the precinct every day is not helping anyone. All the proper information has been passed out to the folks at the command headquarters and they've been advised to keep their eyes and ears open. Anyone—including you of course, who has information on this case can call me day or night."

Realizing that any further argument would be futile, Edward collapsed back in his swivel chair, pinching the bridge of his nose.

"Sergeant, I can't…"

"Call me Rod.

"Rod, man I can't thank you enough."

"It's my job. Hey look I'll let you know if I hear anything. Be well."

Edward placed the phone back in the cradle no more certain of what the outcome would be than he was ten minutes ago. No solid leads has materialized as yet, either from the Sergeant or his efforts. Sure, he knew Sergeant Williams was doing his best, but to sit back and wait for someone else to bring his wife back was unacceptable. He had to do something. He had no idea at this point what that something was, but he would keep looking for his wife until he found out exactly what happened.

Edward knew there had to be something more behind all of this. Like peeling the layers of skin on an onion, he knew there had to be more layers to this case than what was being revealed now. But what? That was the million-dollar question and what would ultimately be the key to finding his wife. Now, as he drove along, not looking forward to going home, he thought about the life he and Mia had shared over the years and was awash by an extreme sense of loneliness. His was an emotional struggle to remain optimistic in the face of overwhelming and almost certain tragedy. Because Mia had grown up as an only child raised by a single mother and her mother had died over three years ago, Edward didn't have the burden of possibly having to break the bad news to any of her family members except a few aunts. However, although he too was an only child, and had no siblings to share his pain with, he was still unwilling to have his parents share the burden of this emotional tragedy.

His mother and Mia had always gotten along extremely well and to break the news to her would be like telling her that her very own daughter was missing. He would rather deal with this on his own, at least for now.

As Edward pulled up to the driveway of his home, he noticed Lynda's Landcruiser parked in front. He checked his watch; it was almost 8:30 p.m. As he exited the car, Lynda had already made her way around the neatly manicured lawn and was fast approaching the driveway on his side of the car with a casserole dish in hand.

"Hey, I brought dinner, because I know you won't eat if I don't," she said attempting to lighten the mood.

"You're right. I just have so many things on my mind — food just doesn't seem important. I feel like the simple act of eating is wrong, while my wife is out there unable to get home."

"Mia is a fighter, Edward. We have to believe that she'll be okay," Lynda said.

" I know Mia is a fighter, but we don't know what we're up against here. And, I feel so helpless, I can only take it day by day," Edward responded as he gently placed his hand in the small of Lynda's back and guided her into the dark house. Once inside with the lights on, Lynda slid her coat off and placed it on the coat rack. She then helped Edward out of his suit jacket and placed it on the rack next to hers in the foyer. Familiar with the layout of the kitchen, Lynda located two potholders and placed them in the center of the small breakfast table. In less than two minutes, Lynda had placed the casserole dish on the pot holders and the plates on the table mats next to the forks just as Edward walked in.

"Soup's on," she said with a smile.

"Lynda you really don't have to do this, you know. I can take care of myself."

"Edward I know you can take care of yourself, but so far you haven't. This kitchen is too clean. The only dish in the sink is the one I brought to you full of food two days ago. And between worrying and working, I know that you've either been eating fast food or nothing at all. I know it must be hell for you, but you have to keep your strength up."

Edward blew out an exasperated breath and held up

his hands in mock surrender.

"Okay, okay. Mia always said she could never win an argument with you."

"It's the very least I can do. Mia will be okay, Edward. We have to believe that."

"Well, it does smell delicious," Edward admitted as he patted his stomach and licked his lips at the sight of the cheesy lasagna. Lynda spooned two healthy servings onto his plate and retrieved an untouched green salad from the refrigerator that she'd made during her last visit. She then fixed her plate and joined him at the small table.

"Well, it tastes even better, so eat up."

They shared a rare moment of laughter as they prepared to devour the savory, casserole.

Ten minutes later, Edward had polished off the last of the lasagna. "That was delicious, Lynda," he said, patting his full stomach. "I can't tell you how much I appreciate these wonderful meals. You know you don't have to do this. I know you're Mia's friend and all, but I also know that you have a life."

"Just stop right there," Lynda said holding her hand up. "I've known you two way too long for you to try and give me this polite brush off. Mia has been like a sister to me and I have no doubt in my mind that if I had children, a husband or even a pet, she'd take care of them without giving it a second thought."

"You're probably right. That was the type of person—I mean is," Edward managed, biting down hard on his lip. "That *is* the type of person she is."

Lynda looked away and there was an awkward moment of silence. "Edward I'm so sorry. I just wish there was more I could do."

"Don't be silly, you were the one who provided the information to the police on this freak whose been at every one of her readings. I'm the one who should've been more aware. This bastard has been at every reading and I never even noticed anyone out of the ordinary. If only I had been more observant. Why didn't she tell me?"

"She didn't want to worry you."

"Worry me!" Edward yelled.

"Don't be so hard on yourself," Lynda offered as she reached across the table and covered Edward's strong hand in both of hers.

"It just makes no sense," Edward shouted, removing his hand from Lynda's. "I was unable to reveal any details as to what the man looked like and I was right in the same damned room."

"Don't do this to yourself, Edward. Many times we both were in the same room and never noticed anything out of the ordinary. I've been asking people if they noticed anyone suspicious during Mia's last book signing at the store. Unfortunately, no one has remembered a thing."

Edward turned from facing the magnetic picture of he and Mia that hung on the freezer door. He squinted to clear his vision as if he'd been on a long journey to the unknown and just recently returned.

"Edward are you all right?" Lynda asked with concern.

"I'm okay. Just tired I guess. I've been having this same dream."

"About Mia?"

"Yeah, but not how you'd think. Usually I'm driving down the street and I imagine I see Mia walking along with this faceless man. Although I never really see her, I know it's her—I just know it. I pull my car over and get out in pursuit of her, but the faceless man knows I'm coming without ever looking back. He pulls her along. As slow as they seem to be running, I can never catch up with them. I get within inches of reaching Mia's arm and she turns and looks at me, but the faceless man continues to pull her like a rag doll." Edward shook his head and rubbed his eyes. "I awaken breathless—my heart hammering so hard in my chest I think it's going to burst."

"Oh, Edward I'm so sorry."

"Yet the most unsettling part of it is not the dream, but the haunted, vacant look in Mia's eyes. That look stays with me throughout the day and drives me crazy unless I'm doing something to help find her."

Lynda shook her head. For once, she was speechless and helpless to offer support. No amount of cooking was going to fill this void for Edward.

"Hey look, I don't mean to lay all this on you. You've been a constant source of support. If it were not for you, I probably would've never gone back to work. I'll never be able to repay you."

"Well, like I told you, no good would come from you running yourself ragged back and forth between the command headquarters and the precinct. I'm confident we'll all get through this and Mia will be all right."

"I keep telling myself that. *But now I just have to make myself believe it,*" he thought.

###

Edward and Lynda relaxed at the small kitchen table over a bottle of Chianti. Edward's favorite spot in the house after a delicious meal used to be the den. It was there that he would snuggle with or make love to his wife and they would fall asleep in each other's arms. Now, to go there seemed disrespectful, an abomination to their marriage. As Lynda had said, he knew Mia was a fighter, but who knew what she was up against. Not even the police had any solid leads as of yet. Lynda was trying as best she could to keep Edward on track, focused and healthy during this entire ordeal and he greatly appreciated that, but she was not Mia and the void left in his life would never be filled until her return.

"So, has the sergeant learned of any new developments in the case?" Lynda asked breaking Edward's reverie.

"No, nothing yet, but with the information you gave them, they're hoping to develop some solid leads soon. I just hope soon is soon enough."

Lynda reached out and gently patted Edward's arm, "It will be okay, don't worry. This just seems like something that happens to *other* people. I mean you see it on the news all the time, but you never think it'll happen to you or someone you know. This entire situation is such a nightmare," Lynda said forcing back tears.

"I know. I just feel so helpless, like I've failed her in some way. As her husband, it is my responsibility to protect her," Edward looked away, unable to meet Lynda's gaze. "But I didn't," he said with finality. He then slammed his fist on the table in frustration rattling the partially empty wineglasses. "And dammit, I should have taken that trip with her," he continued. "I can promise you things would have been different."

"Edward, don't do this to yourself," Lynda spoke carefully dabbing at her eyes as she gathered Edward's large hand in hers. "You don't know how things would have been. And, you have to believe that this will work out and that Mia will be okay." He was thankful for the consolation and the contact that made him feel less alone and isolated than before. But before he began to further analyze these feelings, he quickly removed his hand from her embrace, suddenly uncomfortable with the way it made him feel.

"You're right, we just have to go over every possibility again and again. We're sure to have missed something. I really wish she had told me about this guy when she first noticed him or when his presence began to bother her."

"Hmmm," Lynda muttered as she stood and began clearing the table. "That makes me think of a conversation we had after her last reading at my book store. She began telling me that she had noticed this guy in the audience again and my response to her was that she had many fans and so on and so forth. But, I think that may just be what he is, a fan."

"Mia may have been on to something, Lynda, however, if he is a fan, then he is definitely obsessed and persistant. That possibility scares me. And, the fact that Mia's books appeal to such a wide variety of people only complicates matters, because at a reading you can't tell who looks out of place and who doesn't."

"Yeah, you're right," Lynda said absently as she rinsed the dishes and placed them in the dishwasher.

"What are you thinking?"

"I just thought about the roll of film that I never had developed. It has several different author appearances on it and I'm sure I snapped a few shots of Mia when she was there."

"That's right. I do remember people taking pictures and light bulbs flashing, but I didn't know you had taken any. This is great," Edward said as a glimmer of hope danced behind his beautiful, brown eyes. "Where is the film?"

Lynda chewed thoughtfully on her bottom lip, "If I remember correctly, it's in the glove compartment of my truck," her excitement growing at the possibility. "Since we're all done here, I'll drop it by the nearest Walgreens and it should be ready sometime tomorrow afternoon."

Lynda retrieved her coat from the rack and Edward helped her into it. She turned to face Edward's extended hand, "Lynda thank you ...for everything. Dinner was wonderful and if we can find something in those pictures maybe we can begin to make some progress on this thing. I'm going to call Sergeant Williams and give him the good news."

"What is this handshake stuff about?" Lynda asked, her hazel eyes meeting his steady gaze. She then gathered Edward's handsome face in her hands and planted a petal-soft kiss on his cheek; closer to his lips than was necessary. Edward nervously cleared his throat and took a step back, "Okay. So we'll touch base tomorrow," he said opening the front door.

"Definitely," Lynda replied as she strolled down the walkway and climbed into her truck.

After delivering the roll of film to Walgreens, Lynda decided to take the long way home. The night was cool, but she was hotter than an oven. She turned the air conditioning up an extra notch. Maybe the drive would give her some time to think about and sort through the weird feelings she had been having. She turned up the music and allowed Brian McKnight to serenade her. The clear, beautiful night was a night meant for lovers. Lynda glanced up at the lovely, pristine homes and wondered about the people in them. Were they single or couples? Married, widowed? Did they have someone to keep them company?

She came to a stoplight and watched as a young

couple walking their dog crossed the street. They held each other around the waist as her head rested on his chest. Lynda stared as the couple reached the sidewalk and paused to kiss. *They were laying on a remote beach in Maui clad in only their bathing suits. A warm, gentle breeze blew in from the tropics that seemed to kiss their skin. The golden sun, still shone warmly as it rested just above the surface of the ocean, radiating its golden, orange hues. Edward leaned over and placed a petal-soft kiss on her lips, sending goosebumps shimmying down her spine. He cupped her face in his hands as the intensity of their kiss grew. She sighed in response to his touch and parted her lips slightly, beckoning, urging, demanding that his tongue enter. When it did, it was explosive and the earth beneath her seemed to quake. She reached out and grabbed his neck, pulling him to her, not wanting to allow any breathable space between them. He cupped one of her firm, full breasts and the nipple hardened in answer, stretching against the already tight fabric. His hands traveled the length of her body and....*

The blaring horn roused Lynda from her fantasy. She made a left at the light and drove the three-mile drive past the Marinas. The cattails blew sensually in the wind along the marsh. Lynda breathed deeply.

In his vulnerability, Lynda had become inexplicably more drawn toward Edward. Lynda, Mia and Edward had been friends for many, many years and it was no secret that Edward was an extremely attractive man. What had become a secret throughout Mia and Lynda's many conversations were why Lynda would never give any man half a chance to get close to her. Lynda would always tell Mia that it was because she didn't have the time it required to nurture a relationship. That she was much too busy trying to get her life together and secure her own future to complicate matters right now. Sure, Mia knew of her bad relationships with men who had used her sexually and financially or wanted a trophy on their arm. But, what she never confided to her

friend was that her perception of the perfect man was in fact
her husband, Edward Simone. From the first time Mia intro-
duced her to him, it had been a battle of wills to keep her
emotions at bay. She would always appear nonchalant on
the outside, in their presence, but her insides were doing
flip-flops and a warm sensation would start at the top of her
head and end between her legs.

Lynda had never before entertained the thought of
crossing the line with her best friend's husband, it was
unconscionable. Yet Mia had always been there when they
were around each other, now she wasn't, and that was the
only conclusion Lynda could fathom for the wicked thoughts
she'd been having. In the few days Mia had been missing,
it seemed that Edward's maleness was becoming increasing
prevalent to Lynda. There was something electric there that
made her pulse quicken whenever they caught each other's
gaze. His cologne had become a complete aphrodisiac and
she viewed him as a man — a very sexy man—instead of
just her friend's husband. *What is going on with me? How
could I possibly be thinking about something like this at such
a grievous time?* Lynda thought, but could not easily dismiss
the notion. For a fraction of a second this evening, she *knew*
Edward was feeling something too, when she looked into his
dark, deep eyes. There was something behind them other
than excitement about something that could possibly help
the case; there was fire, passion and a familiar attraction that
Lynda had seen in the eyes of many, many men. She would
find out tomorrow if her intuition was right.

Maybe I should give Michael a call, she thought. *I
need a diversion.*

Chapter Nine

Mia sat confined to the four-legged wooden chair, facing the door of the poorly kept, mildew-smelling motor home. She wondered when and if she would ever see Edward again. These thoughts had plagued her daily since she had been made privy to the madness and obsessions of her captor. She absently fingered the small knot on her forehead from two days ago and was reminded of a debate she had seen years ago on a late night talk show. The topic was whether to fight back or not when in a dangerous situation, like attempted rape or kidnapping. Mia had always thought that the right answer was definitely to fight back, what other alternative was there at that point? She scoffed at women who submitted to their attacker's every whim only to be used at their disposal, discarded like garbage and left with the guilt of "what if?" Yet, fighting back had gotten her nowhere. It did leave her unconscious and with a large knot on her head, but it hadn't gotten her killed either. Once she regained consciousness, she and her captor came to an understanding — that as long as she behaved and didn't try to escape, he would not hurt her. Fortunately, she believed him when he told her that he was not going to rape her, from the psychology books she'd read, his behavior did not suggest such. But she was not a psychologist and could not clearly read what his behavior suggested as it related to the bigger picture; other than there was deep, unidentifiable, emotional issues. She also knew that when he reached his boiling point or mental plateau, she didn't want to be anywhere within breathing space of him. No matter what the textbooks might say, this guy was as crazy as they came. Over the past few days, he had begun calling her Valerie Lassiter, which was the character in her book. If he was in fact attempting to play out the events of *A State of Mind*, Mia knew that her situation was growing more dire by the day.

However, what had Mia thrown off was the fact that he was not following the details of the book to the latter, but rather implementing his own distorted nuances to it as he went along. This made it difficult for her to predict his next move.

Mia looked down at the handcuffs on her hands and the abrasions encompassing her wrists that had begun to bleed again. Her eyes roamed the length of her body. Her left arm revealed a neat trail of four cigarette burns, all of which had been administered when Mia spoke out of turn, raised her voice or used profane language. This was his form of punishment. Mia had never known such torture on a mental or physical level. Since she was a small child, she had never had to choose her words carefully and even then, the punishment was nothing like this. Her eyes reluctantly left her arm and scanned the length of her body. The once beautiful eggplant-colored pantsuit was now filthy, stained and torn in several places. Her previously stockinged feet were now shrouded in strips of black nylon fabric. If she angled her body to the right or left, she could see either of her bare feet securely tied to the legs of the chair with rope, as was her torso to the back of the chair.

Splaying her fingers, she studied the dirt under each once neatly manicured, nail. She shifted in her seat. She could smell her body odor as it wafted in her airspace. In the three days she had been shackled or handcuffed to one inanimate object or another, she had been allowed to eat three times a day, use the restroom when she needed to and extended the offer to bathe, which she had refused on every request. *Maggots will engulf my entire being before I make a conscious decision to undress and bathe anywhere in his presence. Least of all, use his soap, towels and anything else other than what is required to sustain my strength when the time comes for me to flee*, she thought bitterly.

The only way she had been able to keep track of the days was because of the steady stack of newspapers that Parker had allowed to accumulate inside the already filthy mobile home, obviously looking for something regarding her disappearance.

Because she could only see the top page of the newspapers and only enough to read the date, she knew two things, one; that her case had not made headlines and two; that they were still in the Los Angeles area. Her heart was heavy with the thought of what her husband must be going through. Edward being the type of person he was, most likely had not told his parents just yet, especially his mother. It was not uncommon for him to go without speaking to them for two to three weeks at a time and he certainly would not want to worry them prematurely. They knew she would be on tour, but had no idea when she would return.

Her eyes carefully traveled the length of her hands and arms, acutely aware of the cuts and bruises when she noticed that the face of her Cartier watch had been cracked and the hour hand was missing. The only object on her that remained in tact was her wedding ring. The 2.5-Carat, pear-shaped beauty seemed to sparkle like a beacon in the night, navigating a lone ship to safety. Mia's eyes teared as her thoughts carried her back to her wedding on a beautiful June day almost six years ago. It had been a beautiful wedding with seventy-five people, three of her aunts and numerous business associates of both she and Edward. The remainder of the guests were Edward's family, friends and co-workers. Her dress was a Vera Wang original made of a beautiful eggshell white organza with a strapless, pleated bodice trimmed with beaded embroidery and a chapel train.

The sound of footfalls crunching on gravel abruptly brought Mia out of her reverie. She rotated one of her wrists to alleviate some of the stiffness and winced in pain as the handcuffs scraped yet another scab, causing it to bleed.

Since their encounter days ago, some semblance of respect had been established, but Mia couldn't help her feeling of anxiety. Now that her blindfold had been removed,

Mia noticed that her abductor now walked about the tiny dwelling comfortable with having her know who he was— that he had been stalking her all this time. He'd had a beard then, but he confided in her that the only reason he shaved it was to elude police when he went into the city to buy essentials.

"I really respect the fact that we can talk now, Mia," he had confided. "I knew that you knew who I was—what my motives and intentions were from the start. It was only a matter of time before you came to your senses."

"And I have come to respect the fact that I'm dealing with a lunatic," was her response.

"You think because I take medicine I'm crazy? Well, you're wrong. These meds," he spoke spraying spittle as he held them both between his thumb and forefinger, "allow me to keep things in perspective is all."

"Well you obviously need a different prescription," Mia chided. The knot on her head had only slowed her down, made her stronger, but it would not stop her. The next time she tried to escape, it would be life or death, whether it was his or hers, would be the deciding factor.

Earlier she had managed to see the prescription on the bottles, one of 300 milligrams of Luvox and the other, 800 milligrams of Novartis and part of his name, *Parker*.

Maybe being able to address him by name would allow him to let his guard down some. From her research, she knew that Luvox was a Fluvoxamine agent for mood disorders and was among a family of anti-depressants such as Prozac, Paxil, Zoloft and Nardil to name a few. And, Novartis was a Thioridazine agent for antipsychotics. Many of them had low to moderate side effects for sedation and high to extremely high side effects for irreversible, retinal pigmentation, sexual dysfunction, including decreased libido and retrograde ejaculation which would explain his lack of interest in raping her. Additionally, because of the sedation from the drugs, he slept most of the day, allowing

Mia ample time to reflect on her situation and observe his daily patterns. Thank God for side effects, she thought taking in a shaky breath. *If only I had told Edward when I first noticed him.*

Mia held her breath as the door knob slowly turned and Parker stepped up and into the mobile home wearing a baseball cap pulled down low over his eyes. He had a brown knapsack in one hand, with what Mia knew was filled with more T.V. dinners, a dog-eared copy of her book, *A State of Mind* and a newspaper tucked under his arm.

Mia exhaled, suddenly aware that she had been holding her breath. Parker looked to be between 29 to 32 years of age, 5'7 to 5'8 maximum with thin, brown hair. And, of course he now possessed no hair on his face. Because he was rail thin, the blue jeans he wore hung on his lithe frame and the lumberjack shirt seemed to swallow him. Her guess was that he weighed no more than 145 pounds soaking wet. There were dark circles under his brown eyes—like he was suffering from anorexia nervosa. His skin looked more pallid than she remembered and she was instantly reminded of pictures she had seen in a magazine on eating disorders. In fact, most of the time he prepared her dinner, he never ate, unless it was candy bars. *This could work to my advantage.*

"Well, good morning Val, did you sleep well? Probably not. Who would sleep well in a chair," Parker rambled on answering his own questions.

"Please don't call me Val. My name is Mia," Mia said evenly. She had learned that please and thank you seemed to go over big with him.

"You know Val, you are really coming along," he said ignoring her request. "You see how much easier it is to be nice and cordial rather than use the foul language you were accustomed to when you came here. I know of your sordid past," he ranted hefting the book in his right hand. "And others like you who are just drifters in this society. We are a lot alike and yet very different," he continued.

"I am not Valerie Lassiter and I was never a teenage runaway who had to turn tricks just for a meal. Valerie is a fictional character. Why can't you understand that?" Mia pleaded.

Over the past few days, he had been using direct quotes from her book, yet he would use it totally out of context in reference to her, or rather Valerie Lassiter.

"What I understand is that we can not run away from who we really are. You are an irresponsible whore and a liar just like my mother was. But, I will rid you of your old self no matter what it takes. I've covered our trail and destroyed your last link with the material world," Parker said as he pulled up a folding chair and sat directly opposite Mia. "Because deep down, I know that you are sweet, pure and understanding—everything I need you to be...my beloved Valerie," he slurred as his eyes glazed over and he began to nod, the effects of his medication taking an unusually strong hold of him.

What the hell does that mean?, Mia thought frantically. "No," she screamed at the top of her lungs, bringing Parker fully alert. He immediately jumped from his chair, toppling it over in the process. He stomped over to the cabinet above the tiny sink where the cigarettes were kept. She knew this time would be no different than the rest as he retrieved the pack from an old coffee can. Mia screamed a succession of 'No's' until they became a mantra, but to no avail. With an iron grip, Parker held her arm steady as he slowly brought the cigarette to within inches of her skin.

"Now," he said. "Don't you wish you'd thought before screaming at me like that?" Closer, the lighted tip edged toward her straining arm. Simultaneously, the pain and the smell of her own flesh burning, caused bile to rise in her throat. She choked back the bitter taste as a scream caught in her chest and restricted her breathing. She would not let him break her.

As if she had been encapsulated in a time machine, she was thrust back to her teenage years when she earned her brown belt in Karate. She had been the only person of color in her class and had struggled to master every Kata to earn her next belt. On this particular day, she was going up to be promoted for her next belt. She had been through many promotionals, but today was different—she was scared to death. Suddenly, out of nowhere, her Sensei's voice reverberated in her head...*Makuso*. She closed her eyes and slowed her breathing. This was the Japanese word her instructor would use before she told them to allow their bodies and mind to become one and block out the pain—block out the burning in their underdeveloped muscles as they held stances.

"This is good for you," her Sensei would assure the class.

In the beginning, Mia's legs would cramp up, but soon, when she thought of the word *Makuso*, her body and mind would not only become one, but her body would go numb and feel empowered by whatever signals her brain sent to it.

Hurled back to the present, Mia whispered a barely audible, *Makuso* and stared her captor right in the eyes as he removed the cigarette from her skin. She knew that things had changed. Her resolve would not be diminished again. Now, she would play his sick little game, but she would play it to win—even if it meant answering to *Valerie*.

"I'm sorry, Parker. I'll be good from now one."

Parker appeared only briefly surprised at the mention of his name. With a slight smile, he responded,

"Valerie, you don't know how long I've waited to hear you say that."

Chapter Ten

Edward pushed the half-full plate of toast and scrambled eggs aside as his stomach turned into knots. Day by day he felt more helpless. Unable to concentrate at work, leaving early every afternoon bone-tired, with the intention of finishing up at home had become routine. Instead, today he would head straight to the precinct to learn of any possible new developments and offer help wherever he could. Although it had been close to a week since her disappearance, he still had not informed his mother of what was going on. He hoped he was doing the right thing. Mia was just like a daughter to her, but he just didn't feel it necessary to cause alarm, yet. If nothing broke in the next week, he would have to make the call. Most likely she would assume that Mia was still on tour and he had gone with her— unless she had seen it on the news. Even after spending all her life in New Orleans, Louisiana, Mrs. Dorothy Simone was never without something to do. Between the Mardi Gras and other spectacular events there, she and his dad were far more active than he and Mia would ever be. However, thankfully they spent most of their time in church and traveling.

The case had made all the local newspapers and television stations, but he wasn't sure if it had gone national. He was still painfully optimistic that Mia was still alive even though there had been no solid leads as yet. Many callers had phoned in to the command center reporting that they had seen Mia on the last day of her tour. However, most of them were from San Francisco and had seen her before she even boarded the plane. This information had not proven useful, as Edward and the police had already confirmed Mia on the flight from SFO to LAX. From the time of debarkation is where she seemed to vanish into thin air. There had been one major development in the case. The roll of film that Lynda had developed produced one small but clear image of a late twenty to early thirty-year old man with brown hair and a full, brown, scruffy beard sitting in the last row of seats in the bookstore. At first glance, there seemed to be nothing outwardly suspicious about his presence except that he was a little disheveled looking. But eight of the twenty-four pictures Lynda had taken at Mia's last booksigning at her store, basically created a step-by-step visual of the event unfolding from beginning to end. The first four pictures looked almost identical. The man is in the same seat in every picture, the only differences are the movements of the people around him. One woman is scratching her head, another is looking at the camera and a third has her head angled slightly different from the other three previous pictures. The next three pictures show the audience stirring to get in line to have their books autographed—again, the man is sitting there and he's the only one. In the last picture, people are having their books signed and in the far left corner of the picture that showed him, the man can be seen as he walked out of the bookstore.

Edward placed the pictures on the nightstand. He had provided copies and the proofs to Sergeant Williams two days ago so that their lab technician could construct a large 8 x 10 photo. From there, they would have a sketch artist draw up a composite from the 8 x 10. These were scheduled to be complete yesterday. As Edward lay across the king-sized, four poster bed waiting for the promised call from Sergeant Williams to come to the station, his mind wandered. Staring out the picture window, he marveled at how calm the beautiful, blue sky appeared. He could hear birds chirping and the neighbor's dog barking two houses down as the block began to come alive with the new day. He rolled onto his side, sick with the thought of how easily life went on no matter what the tragedy was and who it was happening to.

He sat up on the edge of the bed thinking of the number of times he had slept alone since he and Mia had been married. There had been quite a few between his business travels and Mia's book tours, but there had never been a time when the loneliness had been so profoundly debilitating. He laughed to himself as he absently clutched the forest green, paisley print comforter. Mia had teased him about their never reaching the bedroom whenever they made love. The truth was that they had christened every room in the house, but the bedroom was usually a part of their morning sessions, whereas, the family room was where they had heated up a lot of evenings.

Edward stood and crossed the large master bedroom to the elegant bathroom with its double sinks, huge oval bathtub and separate shower. He took a cursory glance at all the sparkling fixtures. Mia had painstakingly chosen every tile, fixture and wallpaper pattern that had gone into making this house a home. They knew that they would never move from here. The house had been conveniently located, beautifully priced and the perfect size for the family they planned to start after Mia's tour. So many evenings as he had pulled into his driveway almost too tired to get out the car, his home and the warm, proud glow on Mia's face were a glorious reminder of why he worked so hard. This morning, the house seemed cold, sterile and ominous. He continued to allow the maid to come once a week to scrub away all traces of the mess his life had become.

He stared at the reflection in the mirror and ran a large, chocolate-colored hand across his dark, silky waves. Turning his face from side to side to evaluate the new growth of razor stubble, he opted to forgo a shave for the day. He removed his T-shirt and boxers and stepped on to the cool porcelain tiles in the glass shower. Hot water pelted his chest and ran down his sculpted body. Plumes of thick, misty smoke swirled to the top of the ceiling and disappeared between the blades of the black ceiling fan. The water continued its assault on the taut muscles in his back and shoulders as he dipped his head slightly, allowing it to run over him and sluice some of the tension and worry away.

Upon exiting the shower, he heard the phone ringing. He grabbed a bath towel hanging from one of the two brass hoops on the wall just outside the shower and made his way into the bedroom. Catching the phone on the third ring, he snatched up the portable handset and said, "Hello."

"Hello, Edward Simone?   This is Sergeant Williams." Edward suddenly felt weak and unsure that his muscular legs would support him. He wrapped the towel tightly around his waist, cinched it at the side and took a seat on the edge of the bed. He had been expecting this call, but there was something in the Sergeant's voice that he couldn't make out and it made him feel anxious.

"Hey, Sergeant Williams. Any news—new leads?"

"There's been what could be interpreted as a lead from the photos given to us by Ms. Hastings."

"Yeah?" he asked in a shaky voice as he picked up a handgrip and began to squeeze furiously.

"Yeah, we were able to get a positive identification of this guy from the photos. Now, we just need to see if anyone recognizes him or can place him at more than one of your wife's events."

"Do you have a name yet?"

"As a matter of fact we do. Dr. Fischer provided that to us when she was shown the photos. His name is Parker McKinley.

"Who?"

"Parker McKinley. He's the guy we want to talk to about your wife."

"Well who is he? Does he have a record?"

"We've found nothing on him. Of course, this will make our search a little more difficult."

"Parker McKinley," Edward said as if saying the name would help him get closer to finding Mia. "Well, that's the first good news I've heard," Edward breathed deeply.

"It's excellent news," the Sergeant answered in an upbeat voice that Edward wasn't sure he'd ever heard from him before. He relaxed a bit and released his hold on the handgrip.

"Really?"

"Yes it is. We have one of the best composite sketch specialists in the state working right here. He can take a spec from a film and tell you what it is. We can take the composite to the newspapers and let them have a ball. With his face on television and in the papers, we're bound to flush him or whomever knows something about the case out of the woodwork."

"Finally, we're making some progress," Edward whispered, pinching the bridge of his nose.

"Yes. And, thanks to Dr. Fischer we easily obtained a name to a lead. She had been gone for the week-end to a medical convention in Baltimore. Upon her return, she was shocked to learn the news about Mia's disappear-ance. She told me that Mia had been to her office to do some research last month, just as you said."

Edward remembered that day well because he had dropped Mia off at the appointment. He sighed heavily as if thinking about it brought him physical pain.

Sergeant Williams continued, "The information given by Dr. Fischer was given in strict confidence and with the understanding that her name and the name of her prac-tice and its partners not be revealed. Understandably, the information she gave can only be used as a psychological profile and nothing else. What her information revealed is confirmation that Mia may be in the hands of a very dis-turbed individual if Mr. McKinley is in anyway involved in the case."

This did nothing to allay Edward's fears. His stomach knot-ted.

Sensing his hesitation, Sergeant Williams contin-ued on. "So, in layman's terms Parker McKinley is an obsessive-compulsive with major psychological problems. Unfortunately, as stipulated by the law, Dr. Fischer cited the doctor-patient priveledge, and is really not at liberty to discuss any of her patients files. Although, she stopped treating him over a year ago, the laws still apply. She's not sure who he was referred to or if he's even seeing a psychologist now."

"I don't believe it, mental patients and criminals have more rights than everyday working-class citizens," Edward said, his voice reaching a frenzied pitch.

"It's not as bad as it appears. You have to remember that all of this, up to this point, is just circumstantial. We have nothing on this guy yet, we just want to talk to him. He may have nothing to do with Mia's disappearance."

"Yeah, I was afraid you'd say that, but we still need to find him and make sure."

"We're going to do that, but the best thing we can do is what we've been doing. We're racing against the clock, but we just have to beat the clock."

"Yeah. Well I guess having a name helps."

"Yeah, but just a little bit. We still have a long way to go and a lot to do. We've turned up nothing on this Parker McKinley, so more than likely the guy doesn't have a record. But I'm optimistic that once the public sees the photos, our phones here and at your command center will start ringing off the hook."

"So what's the next step?"

"Our next step is to do a press conference and get these pictures and his name out there. Someone has to have seen something or know something. In the interim, we continue looking for clues and anything else that might be essential to the case."

"And to encourage people to come forward, I'll offer a fifty thousand dollar reward."

"I think that's a very good idea. The sooner the better."

"Great. Sergeant Williams thank you for the call. I'll be there within the hour."

"Okay, see you then."

Edward hung up the phone feeling lighter in spirit than he had in days. Not bothering to replace the phone to its stand, he cleared the line and dialed his office number. After one ring, his assistant answered, "Kincaid and Blake, Edward Simone's office."

"Hello, Nathalie. This is Edward, how are you?"

"I'm fine Mr. Simone, how are you today?"

"A little better, thank you. I'd like to have you clear my calendar for the day. I don't plan to come in, but I will check in for my messages every couple of hours and of course you have my cell phone number."

"Of course. I'll call you if I need you," she responded.

"Good. Do I have any messages so far?"

"Mr. Blake called from his business trip in Europe, he said he just heard and he'll keep you in his prayers. He will touch base with you upon his return. Other than that, there's nothing that can't wait until you return. Now you take care of yourself."

"I will, Nathalie. Thank you."

Edward disconnected the line, grateful that Nathalie was so knowledgeable about what to do at the office in his absence. She probably knew more than he did about their clients. Edward hired the, forty-something, senior executive assistant three years ago after his previous assistant decided to take early retirement. He thought he would never be able to replace Phyllis Hodge who had been with the company since its inception, but he had. In fact, Nathalie Benson, was ten times sharper than Phyllis had ever been. She was constantly finding ways to enhance the efficiency of her job as well as his and made it a priority to learn the inside workings of the business and its clientele. She was a jewel and Edward knew the office was in very capable hands. Everyone in the firm who wasn't traveling internationally knew about Mia's disappearance and they had been extremely understanding and supportive—even some of the local clients had sent cards and e-mail messages with words of encouragement. Marilyn Kincaid and Stephanie Blake, the wives of the partners, had arranged for the chef at an upscale restaurant in Beverly Hills to prepare and deliver meals nightly to Edward. The exclusive restaurant was co-owned by Mr. Robert Kincaid, the senior partner of the firm.

Edward was impressed by some of the elaborate presentations of these finely packaged meals. But most of them he could neither identify nor pronounce. He was not the ungrateful type, but most of the food was mediocre, at best. The sad part was that this restaurant and its chef had been given the Zagat Award last year. *Humph*, he thought after sampling one of the meals. *If I had to pay for this, I'd be really pissed off.*

Returning the phone back to its stand, Edward stood in front of the large, walk-in closet. He chose a light-weight, beige, T-shirt and khaki, cargo-pants and laid them out on the unmade bed. The grumbling sound in his stomach nearly startled him. He couldn't remember the last time he was actually hungry.

He walked down the hall and descended the spiral staircase to the large, gourmet kitchen. Cereal was a quick fix. Chopping the last of the banana on top of his corn flakes, he added ice-cold milk. No sooner than he put the first spoonful into his mouth, the doorbell sounded.

Surprised to see Lynda peering back at him through the half moon-shaped window set within the heavy, oak door, he opened it with one hand and balanced his bowl of cereal in the other. She was holding a white paper bag that he suspected contained donuts. Edward was taken aback by Lynda's beautiful, flowing auburn hair. He was sure that he'd never seen her wear it down before. He liked it. It defined her features and accentuated her already arresting, hazel eyes.

Lynda's eyes grew wide as she was momentarily mesmerized by Edward's half-naked form. The damp hairs on his chest glistened in the sun giving it a satiny appearance. Her eyes trailed the hairs on his chest down to the contours of his washboard stomach. From there, she fought with her imagination as to what lay beyond the bath towel that was securely tucked and cinched at his waist. Temporarily winning the battle over her rampant imagination, she honed in on his dark features, which seemed accentuated in the light of the golden sun. Lynda seemed to take him all in within moments. Noticing the curly, black lashes, thick eyebrows and full lips, surrounded by a silken goatee, she was carried away into the erotic fantasy she'd had last night.

"Are you coming in here or what?" Lynda heard. The familiar voice was pulling her back to reality. "Where are you?"

Lynda cleared her throat, "Uh, I--I was just thinking about Mia," she lied, sauntering in the house and closing the door behind her. "Well, it looks like I missed breakfast," she shouted to Edward's retreating back as he headed upstairs to the bedroom to dress.

Edward re-appeared within minutes fully clothed and smelling of Cool Water Cologne--Lynda's favorite cologne for men. He was dressed casually, which was an attractive change. Lynda couldn't remember ever seeing him without a suit and tie. She liked the contrast and wickedly thought how she'd love to know what precious cargo he was carrying in those cargo pants. Last night's fantasy began to encroach on her thoughts. *Stop it, Lynda*, she mentally scolded.

"No, not really. Can I offer you some corn flakes," he said returning to his bowl, which he had placed on one of the Corian countertops.

"No thank you. I'll just have to eat both of these sinfully, rich, strawberry filled delicacies I brought." They both laughed. "Any news," she asked pulling out a chair and biting into one of the pastries.

"As a matter of fact, yes." Lynda noticed an unusual sparkle in Edward's eyes and surmised that it must be good news, but she let him continue. She hadn't seen him this upbeat since before Mia's disappearance. "I spoke with Sergeant Williams about fifteen minutes ago. That's where I'm headed now. They were able to produce a clear image from the negatives of the pictures you took and have come up with a name, Parker McKinley," Edward said with contempt. "They are also drawing up a composite. I'm going to have a bunch of copies made and leave them at the command center for posting."

"Edward that's great," she said as she stood to give Edward a hug. "I'm so happy to see that some progress is finally being made." Smelling the scent of him, she could have stayed in his arms forever, but reluctantly released her grasp. "But, who the hell is Parker McKinley?"

"Apparently, he's some psycho-fan who can't differentiate reality from fantasy."

"No kidding!"

"But yeah, it is great to have a lead. And thank you, Lynda. Remembering that roll of film is the best thing that has happened in this case so far."

"You're welcome. I would do anything for you and Mia." There was an awkward silence.

"Well, I don't mean to rush you, but I really need to get down to the station. I'm also putting up a $50,000.00 reward. I'm hoping it will encourage people to really try to remember anything unusual that they may have seen."

"I'm sure it'll help," Lynda said as she placed Edward's empty bowl in the sink and disposed of her trash in the trash compactor.

"Let's hope so."

"How are those gourmet dinners coming along? I'm hurt that you no longer require my services," Lynda said playfully. Edward discerned a double meaning and caught a glimpse of her beautiful, hazel eyes and perfectly-shaped lips. He grabbed a soft, brown, leather jacket from the hall closet and put it on.

"Those gourmet dinners are delicious," he lied. Lynda slanted her eyes at him. "But, they don't hold a candle to your home cookin'," he continued as he retrieved Lynda's jacket from the back of the dining room chair and held it for her. She walked into that 'too close' airspace near him again and inhaled that intoxicating cologne. As she wriggled into her black, denim DKNY jacket, she could feel the heat of his hands, his body. She knew it was now or never. She only hoped she could be forgiven for betraying her friend, especially at a time like this.

Lynda spun on her heels, doing a complete three hundred and sixty-degree turn, situating herself directly in front of Edward. Their gazes met and there was fire in them. Without saying a word, they embraced, as if they knew this time would come — had to come. There was hunger, passion; a need to feel connected to something other than sadness and uncertainty. As their kisses ignited a flame of urgency, Edward massaged the fullness of Lynda's overflowing breasts and exposed one of her nipples from beneath the tiny tank top she wore, his hands constantly moving, searching, igniting small fires within her. He suckled the sweet fruit and she moaned in ecstasy, willing to succumb to his every desire. She was swept away once again into her own erotic fantasy...only this time it was real and she would see it to an end.

Chapter Eleven

Mia stood and walked about freely for the first time since she had been in captivity. She had learned to play Parker's sick, little game—but she was winning. Learning the key words, such as please, thank you and answering to Valerie had gained her freedom—to some degree. It had also stopped the cigarette burns. Parker was even learning to trust her— allowing her to move around the cramped dwelling, only confining her before he slept or before he went out. Between the two, she was only free about three hours a day each morning, but the ability to move freely had never been so sweet.

As she played the role of prisoner and maid, heating both their dinners in the microwave, Parker was content snacking on his chocolate candy bars, discarding the wrappers on the floor and sleeping most of the day. Mia wasn't sure if he wanted a wife, mother or just company. When they would have their 'get to know each other' sessions, he would have these long dialogues, as the conversations were always one-sided, referring to her as Valerie.

"Valerie, I know you'll try to escape and that's why I keep you under lock and key," he would explain. "Although I've never killed anyone before, I know it's my destiny—not to kill just anyone, but to kill you, just as it was written."

"In *A State of Mind*, it was never written that Valerie—that I was killed, but could even be assumed by certain readers, depending upon their perception of the outcome, that she—I in fact lived and chose to live out my life with you, rather than risk my family being killed."

"Well, well. I guess my perception was different, Val," Parker sneered, his voice laced with a newfound contempt. Mia knew that she and *Valerie* were running out of time. Of the thirty chapters, he was on chapter twenty-three.

No matter what Mia told him, he would not believe that Valerie Lassiter lived—was a survivor. But, then she had an idea.

"You know Parker, I-I-, Mia has written a sequel." Parker stopped dead in his tracks like he'd just seen a ghost. He then started pacing the floor again, only this time with a fervor she had never seen.

"This changes everything," he mumbled. Mia didn't know what that meant, but she suspected that it bought her some very precious and much needed time.

As Mia's future became increasingly uncertain, she began to practice her Karate in her mind. Even with the lack of daily exercise, her small muscles seemed to stay taut and toned. Going back to when she was fifteen years old, she envisioned herself low in her horse stance, doing her katas with precision, her blocks, punches and kicks, strong and graceful.

"I'm going out, Valerie," the sound of Parker's voice breaking into her meandering thoughts. "So you know what that means."

Mia was clearing the few remaining, plastic dishes out of the sink. She smirked inwardly at the thought of washing all plastic dishes and utensils and wondered briefly if she herself was going crazy, too. Everything was set up to be childproof, now. Since her attempted escape and attack on Parker, she wondered if she had scared him. He had gone out of his way to remove every piece of silverware out of the motorhome. However, he still donned the gash on his face inflicted by her. But, even crazy people have moments of sanity and know the difference between life and death.

Walking to the front of the wooden chair—the only piece of furniture not nailed to the floor of the mobile home— Mia sat, offering no resistance and allowed herself to be tied up, again. The scabs and abrasions had begun to heal after she had been allowed to apply ointment to them. Her wrists and left forearm now looked like they belonged to someone who had led a very hard life, with cigarette burns now totaling six.

She had learned to play the game. Having never been in an abusive relationship, she could only imagine that it must be something very similar to this.

He tied each of her hands to the arm of the chair and bound her feet in what seemed to be less than thirty seconds. Though he had repeated this procedure numerous times, this was the first time Mia had really taken notice of the precision in which he did it—like he must have had some special training or something. Maybe he had been in the Boy Scouts when he was younger or maybe even some military training not so long ago.

"I'll be back," he said thinly, as if suddenly something had upset him and Mia was reminded of the movie, The Terminator. She nodded her head, like a puppy eager for affection, but never said a word. He stood, opened the door and quickly closed it behind him. Mia inhaled and could smell the heat of the hot summer day. She suddenly felt even more melancholy and more alone than ever as she thought about the vacation she and Edward had talked about taking this summer to Ixtapa, Mexico. The rims of her eyes began to sting and she batted her lashes furiously, refusing to give in. She had to stay strong. Surveying the tiny dwelling, she couldn't help but wonder where Parker was going today. There was a weird look in his eyes when he left. Although, he didn't leave every day, when he did, she was thankful for the respite. It gave her a chance to empower herself mentally.

Her eyes slowly closed and color images appeared of herself in full Karate uniform and brown belt. The image of her standing in front of the television screen exercising to her Tae Bo workout video. Mia opened her eyes and as if really seeing for the first time, she spotted a shiny object. It looked like a pair of scissors. The handle just barely stuck out from up under the growing stack of newspapers that

Parker had been collecting. Strangely enough, she noticed that he had not bought a paper in over a week. But she was sure those scissors were meant to be hidden, as were all the other sharp objects that had been done away with.

She would soon be ready to try and get away again, but this time there could be no mistakes...

###

Parker drove his raggedy van into the small town of Palmdale. It was the closest, most obscure town where he was sure he could make it in and out without being noticed. He just needed one more thing before he and Valerie hit the road. Perhaps he hadn't considered the fact that Mia's husband would go to such lengths to ensure her safe return. He glanced again at the newspaper he'd purchased before getting on the road. On the front page was a picture of him with his beard, a composite drawing of what he would look like without his beard and a picture of Mia. Additionally, a $50,000.00 reward was being offered for any information leading to Mia's safe return. Parker flinched. He planned to be gone before anyone had a chance to collect the reward.

"You think you're so smart," he hissed, tossing the paper on the floor of the van on the passenger's side. And then to make matters worse, he had been told that a sequel had been written to the book. *Why wasn't it in stores yet?* In his confusion, he hadn't bothered to ask that question. He'd bet anything she was lying, but she would certainly be put to the test. Parker cut off the engine and got out of the van. Quickly, he entered the pawnshop. Upon scanning the shelves and counters, he soon found what he had come to get.

Mia stiffened when she heard the sound of the vehicle's engine shut off. She had learned to identify the sound, though she had never seen the vehicle or her external surroundings, but knew that there was gravel on the ground. The few hours a week when she was free from the chair, the windows stayed covered. Well aware of the repercussions, she never attempted to lift the dark curtains, which enveloped her in a deeper state of despair.

Parker stormed into the dilapidated Winnebago carrying a partially rusted, battered, old typewriter and a ream of paper. He slammed them down on the small counter near the sink and then narrowed his gaze on Mia.

"You," he hissed in an accusatory tone. "claim to have written a sequel. Why isn't it out? I haven't seen it in bookstores—not even advertised. What do you have to say for yourself?"

"I did," Mia said swallowing the lump of fear in her throat.

"I did," Parker said mocking her. "Is that all you have to say. Like that's suppose to make me believe you."

"That's because the day you decided to kidnap me, I sent the manuscript to my agent," Mia spat with disgust. "Naturally it would take her a few weeks to review it."

"And then what? It goes to the stores right?"

"*Not quite, Einstein,*" Mia thought, but didn't dare say it. "Not quite," she replied instead, but still regretted her tone. She wasn't sure what might set him off.

"What then? If you sent in your manuscript as you say, then why isn't the book out? Surely your agent believes in your credibility as a writer."

"I just told you—" Mia caught herself and lowered her voice an octave. "These things take time. They have to go to the publishing house and be reviewed by the editor. Then, if there are no changes, it goes to print and that takes even more time."

"I see. Well, it doesn't matter. You think you're so

smart—that you know everything," he said, his tone taunting as he gestured toward the typewriter. "Well, we'll just see about that. You're going to type the sequel for me. I'll consider it a private screening in progress. And, I don't care if you have to make it up as you go along—I just hope you're capable of writing on the fly, because first thing in the morning, we're hittin' the road and Valerie and I are going to live the life we've always wanted."

Mia knew that this man was becoming more delusional by the day. One minute she was Mia the author and the next, Valerie Lassiter, the character and figment of his sick imagination. Although he had alluded to killing Valerie several times, Mia was certain he'd do it. People like him had no problem taking their own life. Another persons wouldn't make one bit of difference.

His dementia and psychosis were worsening, as Mia had witnessed the deterioration at an alarming rate over the past week. Initially there had seemed to be some sort of pattern, but now his outbursts were more erratic and more frequent.

"What do you mean? Where are we going?"

"I think you have more important things to worry about, don't you?"

Mia knew that her question had been perceived as rhetorical and didn't expect to be told where they were going. *Where is this coming from? What brought on the need to flee?* She thought frantically. Just when there appeared to be some progress being made. She swallowed hard to rid the lump of fear in her throat. "What is my dead-line?" she managed with as much bravado as she could muster.

"Always the professional aren't you? I knew that about you from the first time I heard you read." Suddenly, his eyes glazed over and Mia realized that he had slipped deeper into that dark place in his psyche where their realities were not the same. When he spoke, his voice was different, slightly lower, as if he had to reach into the deepest bowels of hell to bring forth this particular evil. "Your deadline is whenever I say. For now, just type like your life depended on it."

He quickly retrieved the folding chair, sat the typewriter on it and plugged it into an extension cord that was being powered by the cigarette lighter. He turned his back to Mia and then, almost as if it were an afterthought, he looked over his shoulder and said, "Hmmm, I guess it does. You type, I drive."

With that he sprawled out on the pullout cot fully clothed. He began to nod like a heroin addict and soon fell into a deep slumber. Mia had become desensitized and less repulsed by the disgusting image she witnessed daily.

These were both the best and the worst of times. The best because it was quiet and she could be left alone with her thoughts and didn't have to worry about what type of psychological or physical abuse she would have to endure. The worst because it was quiet and the loneliness was tangible enough to feel, her thoughts plagued with visions of her husband's handsome face, his touch, his smell. Worse, she didn't know how this abuse would end, what her future would be.

Hot tears brimmed in her eyes, clouding her vision. She bit down on her lip to stave off the imminent onslaught, but lost the battle within moments. The dam burst and the brimming tears flowed freely down her cheeks. The salty water briefly touching her lips and falling into her lap. The thought occurred to her to just scream—to keep screaming and never stop, no matter what the repercussions. But given the fact that she had no idea of what her surroundings were like, that thought was quickly replaced with another, *Who Would Hear Her Screams,* anyway.

Chapter Twelve

Edward stared at the rows and rows of numbers displayed on the screen. They all seemed to be a blur. He saved the Excel spreadsheet document and logged out of his computer but remained slumped in the high-back, leather chair. He rotated his neck and shoulders to loosen the stiff muscles from several hours of typing and began thinking of all that had happened.

His thoughts drifted like billows of smoke as Edward sat riveted to his chair. Telling his mother the news about Mia had been the hardest thing he had ever had to do. She had taken the news very hard. In fact, she handled it so badly that Edward thought he was going to have to catch the first flight out to Louisiana. After about forty minutes of crying and praying into the phone, he felt convinced that she would be okay and vowed to her that he would find Mia. As he hung up the phone, he hoped that was a promise he could keep.

Each lead and development had all turned into dead ends and the police were still no closer to finding Mia or the person or persons involved. They seemed to take pride in the fact that they were sure there was foul play involved, but he had known that all along. He had been telling them from the beginning that something had happened to her—and it was not of her own volition. Every time he thought about someone holding his wife against her will and the possible motive or circumstances surrounding it, it made him sick to his stomach.

It had been over a week now and Edward knew the odds of his wife returning home to him were slim and none. That startling reality chilled him to the core and rocked the very foundation upon which his beliefs had been built. But even more frightening was how his life had begun to take on some sense of normalcy under such horrific circumstances.

How could his life ever really be normal again, he wondered. After being off for a few days, he had decided to
return to work. The waiting had nearly driven him mad.
The information was trickling in much too slowly for him to
sit around and wait. Although, some progress had been
made, it simply hadn't been substantial enough to bring his
wife back to him.

Several encouraging pieces of information had
been brought to the attention of the police after the press
conference. Sergeant Williams had obtained a list of the
names of all the passengers that were on the flight with Mia.
Initially, that didn't seem to be very relevant, until a witness
came forth who said he remembered seeing Mia on the flight
and had actually sat next to the man shown on the composite.

"The guy was weird or on something," the witness
had been quoted as saying. He was sure that they did not
exit the plane together because Mia did not appear to recognize anyone on the plane. Additionally, the parking garage
attendant where Mia had parked her car, remembered seeing
a black Lexus the same make and model as Mia's and a man
that fit the description of Parker McKinley behind the wheel,
which would establish Parker McKinley as a suspect. This
development made Edward happy, at least now responsible
or not, he had a face to focus his vengeance on. It had
already been surmised that whatever happened had taken
place inside the parking garage. Unfortunately, the garage
was not equipped with surveillance cameras either. If it had
been, Edward was sure this would never have happened.
The $50,000.00 reward had been set up to be paid to anyone
who provided information that led to the arrest and capture
of Mia's abductor and/or the safe return of Mia Simone. He
would gladly double it and give everything else he had that
was of any worth to have his wife home again. But for now,
the money sat untouched in his bank account. As far as
Edward could tell and after conferring with Sergeant

Williams, they were doing everything right. It just never seemed to be enough.

However, early this morning two more pieces of vital information had come in. Mia's Lexus had been found near a junkyard in East Los Angeles completely stripped. There were numerous fingerprints throughout the vehicle and many had been identified and matched to small-time felons who had been arrested for auto theft. But, the police were certain that the car had been left there to throw them off the trail and make Mia's disappearance look like a mere car jacking. The most they had on the people whose prints were lifted was petty theft, but even the police couldn't prove that the parts had not been taken prior to the car appearing near the junkyard.

This was too generic and not satisfactory for Edward. He cursed under his breath and broke his pencil in two. *And why did that Dr. Fischer even bother calling?* he thought bitterly. She hadn't provided anything really. According to Sergeant Williams, she confirmed Parker McKinley's name, gave a scanty psyche profile that could apply to half of Los Angeles and wouldn't even give his last known address. It was almost like teasing them with the information she had. Edward rubbed his forehead in frustration. Something more had to be done. He pressed the intercom button on his smoke, gray Lucent phone. A voice answered, "Yes, Mr. Simone?"

"Nathalie can you come to my office for a moment," Edward responded. Not waiting for her reply he depressed the button. He was going to have to pull out all the stops, but he needed help from someone he knew was on his side.

Edward drove along the winding Los Angeles free-ways with both windows down. The cool air rushed in through both windows and caressed his face. He inhaled and closed his eyes briefly, imagining that it was Mia's gentle touch and for the slightest moment, he could smell her perfume. For the first time since Mia had been missing, he felt like he was in control of doing something that might produce some tangible results. He opened his eyes and found himself quickly approaching a collision with the vehicle in front of him. Without thinking, he swerved violently to the right with horns blaring in the distance and stopped haphazardly on the shoulder of the freeway. Luckily, traffic was light and he was able to avoid an accident with any other vehicles. He sat there for a moment grateful that no one had been injured, as several passerby's who had witnessed the incident a few cars back, yelled obscenities at him. *What good would I be to Mia if I ended up as road kill?* he thought grimly. He collected his thoughts and eased his Jaguar back into the flow of traffic.

Thinking back to his conversation with Nathalie, a devilish smirk crossed his handsome features. He'd always known that she was a very loyal employee—in fact, the most loyal he ever had. But, what he asked of her had more to do with their friendship and mutual respect for one another rather than an employer-employee relationship. Nathalie had been more than willing to help when he'd asked her to make a phone call first thing in the morning to Dr. Barbara Fischer's office. She would pretend to be the psychiatrist currently treating Parker McKinley and ask to verify his address for a prescription. Using the name of another prominent psychiatrist, she would hopefully obtain the pertinent information they needed from the receptionist—Parker McKinley's address.

He would then go and verify the address first and after making sure it was the correct one, he would notify Sergeant Williams, maybe. He knew what he was doing was probably illegal, but he would just have to worry about that later.

As Edward continued along the freeway toward Sherman Oaks, with the backdrop of Santa Monica in the distance, his thoughts shifted to the last time he'd seen Lynda. *Lynda Hastings, my wife's best friend.* His stomach did a somersault and then settled. What could I have been thinking, he said aloud, but didn't have the answer.

Mentally he relived the events that had taken place a couple of days ago when Lynda had come by. He was elated to be able to share his information with someone—someone else whom he thought loved Mia too—her friend. However, it just seemed to go all downhill from there.

A simple hug ignited something that scared him to death—an urgent kiss and passionate embrace. He could feel the throb of his manhood as he pressed up against Lynda's willing form. He felt her nipples harden in response to him as he took one of her jutting breasts and brought it to his tongue. Yet in the throes of passion, a picture of Mia which sat on the mantle above the fireplace, seemed to stand out more than usual. The simple headshot photo of her with her hair flowing around her beautiful features and a sassy grin on her face, was now a look of hurt. Her eyes filled with accusation and blame. Before things got any more out of his control, he had been able to break free from Lynda's embrace. But, not before she faced him clad in only her black garter belt. Her normally upswept, auburn hair fell, free-flowing past her shoulders. She was a vision that would have made any man in the same situation, cast aside their doubts, guilt and marriage vows. The thoughts and guilt had been weighing as heavily as an anvil on his back. He couldn't understand where those emotions had come from and most of all why they had chosen to reveal themselves now. In all the years Lynda and Mia had been friends, he had never thought of Lynda in a sexual way. In fact, he never thought of any of Mia's friends in that way. Sure, he as well as any man could see that Lynda was a very attractive woman, but he loved Mia and would never deliberately hurt her or disrespect her in such a way.

Understanding that he didn't need to muddy the waters or complicate matters any further, he had backed off from her and strongly suggested that she not come by the house anymore. If something developed in the case that he felt she should know about, he would call her. He proceeded to tell her how grateful he was to her for making sure he ate well and providing the photos that the police were able to make great use of. But, he could see in her eyes that he did not give her the reaction she expected. She just stared at him as she quickly redressed and twisted her hair back up on her head. She was scorned and that concerned him. He didn't want to ever have to tell Mia something like this. But, he knew that their friendship, if it could ever be rekindled, now hung in the balance. There would always be this precarious situation where she no doubt felt she had something on him. At some point, he hoped that he would be able to look back on all of this with his sanity still intact. He sensed there was something with Lynda that no doubt had been brewing for months, maybe even years, yet had gone totally undetected by him. Deep down, he felt that maybe this would have happened anyway. He was just glad he hadn't given in. But, no matter what the outcome of this situation with Mia, he wasn't sure if he'd ever be able to look Lynda in the face again.

He turned left onto his block and relished the serenity of the community. As he approached and stopped in the driveway of his house—the house he and Mia had picked out and shared so many wonderful times together, he thought of what his life would be like without her. He switched off the engine and sat solemnly pondering that question, his mind a blank. Mia was still alive and he knew it. He could feel it in his soul. There was no need to think of what life would be like without her because he was bringing his wife back—back to their home. Some way, he would find her. He opened the manila folder, which sat on the passenger seat of his car and extracted the photo and composite sketch. Switching on the overhead light to view the photo more clearly, he stared at it for a long time, committing it to memory. He looked at the pallid-looking, stranger staring back at him and was surprised that he didn't feel immediate anger. He knew what would happen if he ever came within the same air space of the pale, mountain man looking person on the photo. "And God help you if I get to you first," Edward said as he glared at the photo.

She had been depressed ever since her last visit with Edward. Her thoughts had been nothing more than mass confusion and turmoil. She seemed to be going through life just existing. Her assistant, Gerry, had made it a point to stay out of her way, to the extent of telling her so. "Lynda, if there's anything I can do to help, just let me know. Otherwise, I plan to stay out of your path until this storm blows over," he had told her.

Shaking her head, she thought about just how intolerable she had been. From missing meetings and not returning phone calls to not even bothering to schedule book signing events. Even their usually chatty relationship had been reduced to one-word responses. If she had been him, she probably would have quit by now.

Lynda padded across the bedroom. Standing in front of the full-length mirror, she unfastened her powder blue, silk robe, revealing her nakedness. She couldn't understand what was so wrong with her that men felt she was only good for fulfilling their sexual desires. She knew she looked good. The flawless, honey complexion, arresting, hazel, eyes and perfectly shaped nose. Her full breasts and flat, toned stomach had drawn the attention of many men and women. Turning slightly, she looked over her shoulder and took account of her round, firm bottom.

Gathering the belt and cinching the knot tight around her waist, she slid the mirrored doors open and begin to pick out what she would wear for the day. Yes, she had it together on the outside, but on the inside, she was a mess.

What had she been thinking to throw herself on her best friend's husband. Especially at a time like this. She guessed she was so used to having men throw themselves at her feet, that she was even more attracted to a man who didn't, even if that man belonged to her friend. She was repulsed by her actions. In the heat of the moment, when Edward had responded to her, she felt as light as a feather, like in his arms was where she truly belonged. She felt his arousal and knew that he must be feeling the same way. His kiss was hot, passionate and urgent. Like he had waited for this moment his entire life. The way he suckled her breasts still ignited a welcomed heat between her legs. When he was able to tear himself away, was the most hurtful moment that she could ever remember. She was scorned when she left. In fact, on the drive home, she vowed to destroy his marriage—his life, whether Mia returned or not. But as the crisp, morning air cleared her thinking she knew that what she had done was wrong and that Edward was right to not let things go any further. As someone who had known Mia and Edward for many years, she knew she had not been acting like the person she was suppose to—a friend. In retrospect, maybe that's why she had always been horrible with relationships. She had always been attracted to men who were already in relationships or who weren't mature enough to be in a relationship at all. "Lynda Hastings, this is your life and you'd better get it together," she said grimly. She walked over to her nightstand and pulled out her telephone book. It was filled with the names of men she had dated. Only two women in the entire book, her sister, Gayle and Mia. A single tear trickled, unchecked down her cheek. She flipped back to the B's and looked up Michael Bledsoe. They had dated only a couple of times before she gave him the brush off, afraid that he would be just another number in her book. He seemed to be what she had been searching for, tall, dark, handsome, single and ready for a serious relationship. Maybe she should give him a chance. She sat on the edge of the bed, picked up the phone and slowly began to dial his number.

Chapter Thirteen

Parker drove along Highway 5 making sure he obeyed the speed limit, which was easy to do because of the rain slicked roads. The last thing he needed was to be pulled over by some idiot cop trying to make his quota, he thought morosely. He and Mia had been on the road for an entire day. However, pulling over at the appropriate rest stops had slowed them down considerably. Due to the medication he was taking, he slept a lot and required short intervals of rest in order to stay awake and keep Valerie company.

Parker nodded and then pinched himself hard on the arm to stay alert. In the process, he swerved violently on the slick pavement causing Mia to tumble and bump her head.

"Sorry about that Val. I think it's time to pull over for a rest, don't you?"

"Yeah, I think that's wise," Mia replied.

"I'm glad we agree. 'Ya know I would let you drive but I can't run the risk of Mia taking control. She would only try to convince you to do something stupid, like drive her to a police station," Parker hollered over his shoulder. "Or to her house, where no doubt her husband would be waiting. After all I've been through, that is simply not an option."

Lately, things had become very confusing. Mia and Valerie had been in league with one another almost from the onset to force him to take sides. It was bad enough that he had been having a hard time differentiating the two, but now this.

"We'll pull in at the next rest stop," Parker said drowsily. "You know, in the beginning, I knew in order to get Valerie, I'd have to go through Mia. She was merely the conduit—the host, used to give birth to the life I've longed for with you, Valerie. I cringe at the thought of having had

to follow Mia around to all those readings and book signings, like a little puppy longing for affection. But, it had
been worth it—one dull event after the other. Sure, Mia is
beautiful, but her beauty pales in comparison to yours, Val.
The problem is that Mia is the more dominant personality.
Valerie you have to fight her," Parker said, feeling confident
about his analysis of the situation.

"I've read books about people having multiple personalities. I just hope for your sake there's only two. It's
been quite taxing on me, but I will exorcise this Mia demon
from you if it's the last thing I do, my beloved Valerie."

*He's read about the disorders, but can't apply what
he's learned to himself? What a joke*, she thought. "You're
wrong, Parker," Mia engaged him. "I'm stronger than you
think. Mia only has control over this body when I allow her.
I was just afraid at first."

Mia could see the hopeful look in Parker's eyes as
he glanced back at her from the rear-view mirror.

"And so you're not afraid now, right?"

"That's right. I know I must earn your trust, but
I'm ready to do that."

Parker drove another five minutes in reflective
silence.

"Valerie you are not completely blameless here.
Mia's colorful exploitation of your not-so-perfect childhood
makes me wary of you, at best. Sure you grew up in a sin-
gle-parent environment with only your mother to care for
you. But, you had been well taken care of, unlike myself.
Your father died in an automobile accident when you were
twelve years of age. But what concerns me most Valerie, is
that you never came to terms with your father's death.
Grieving the only way a child knows, you rebelled—ran
away several times, but returned. That makes me hopeful.
But, the last time you ran away, you picked up bad company and a nasty little drug habit that you could only support
by conducting sexual favors. Tsk, tsk, tsk. That's the part

that really sickens me."

How could this nut be so out of it one minute and so acutely aware of finite details the next? "I know and I'm truly sorry. But, I enrolled in a creative writing class in community college which led to my journal and the novel and ultimately…you. Don't you remember?" Mia said, praying her act was convincing.

Even given her past, that Parker dare not think about, he knew she was still a good person. She had come from good stock and he knew he could bring that person back—back to him. They had something in common—a painful childhood. His destiny was to save her from herself. He would not let her make another mistake like that— would not let her turn out like his mother. He'd kill her first, but for now he had to wait and see what this alleged story would say that Mia claimed to have written. She was a master at manipulation and he knew it. He had no doubt that she would try to distort the facts for her own selfish purposes. She really didn't want Valerie to be happy, which was why she had allowed her to go through the torture in the first place. Parker certainly was not going to accept the blame for that. In fact, it was Mia that he was trying to teach the lesson to, not Valerie. In the end, it really didn't matter what Mia wrote. He knew that it was expected of him to stay in the trailer park and be uncertain about whether he'd be captured by the police, but he was smarter than that. They would live on the road if they had to.

Parker smiled as they continued along Highway 5, closely following the road map, which sat on the passenger seat. Once he reached the turn off for 101, he could then follow it into San Francisco and ultimately Las Vegas. When he first got on the road, he was unsure of what their destination would be. But, as he drove along, San Francisco seemed to appeal more and more. It seemed as good a place as any to Parker, for he knew the police would no longer focus their search there. He was certain that they had confirmed Mia's flight from SFO to LAX and confirmed that she was on it. By now, they were most likely combing the Los Angeles area, again.

He knew they would focus on San Francisco for a short while and then re-focus on Los Angeles. A smile formed on his lips as he thought of settling down in Las Vegas. Yes, his life would be different. He had prepared for this time for many months. Steering the van with one hand, he retrieved a half-eaten, chocolate candy bar from the dashboard. He bit into, savoring the chocolatey flavor and slightly accelerated his speed, according to his map, there was a rest stop coming up in a few miles.

The wooden chair to which Mia had been confined had been replaced with a seat on the fold out bed and shackles. The chair she had been seated in was now being used as a desk to support the decaying, ancient typewriter. Having been rid of the chair, she was now able to move about the Winnebago with restricted mobility. Her hands were always bound either by rope or handcuffs and her feet remained shackled. Attached to the shackles was a long, link chain fastened securely around the bottom of the passenger seat of the motorhome. When he slept, she was then remanded back to the wooden chair to sleep, only to wake up with her back throbbing and her neck aching from lack of body support throughout the night. During the days, she spent countless hours memorizing and re-typing the sequel to her book. As she sat crouched over the typewriter, playing a balancing act to prevent the handcuffs from hitting the keys, she thought sadly that maybe she should change the title of this book to, *A Fight for Life*.

The fact that they were on the road further complicated matters and certainly deviated from the storyline of, *A State of Mind*. She didn't know what to expect now. She was fairly certain that re-typing the book had bought her some time and hoped it would give him some direction as to how to proceed with her.

Since they had been on the road, they were in close proximity of one another twenty-four hours a day. In those twenty-four hours, there was not one minute that she was given a respite from her shackles. This would make her escape much more difficult. The menial chore of washing the plastic dishes was no longer hers, it was as if that had been something to help add some sense of normalcy to his life. The same plastic dishes she had been instructed to wash, were now thrown out after their twice-daily meal of lunchmeat, bread, and potato chips. Her job was solely to type and exist to help continue the madness of his personal fantasy. The fact that they were on the go would only prove to make her escape more difficult and make it harder for the police to find a moving target.

Before their journey got underway, Mia peeked through the rear window of the motorhome, watching as Parker pulled an old, van just up behind the Winnebago and hitched the two together. It remained in tow as they traveled along the winding highways. Her mouth dropped open as she remembered seeing the van once before after her last visit to Dr. Fischer's office. He had been stalking her. Although she noticed a man who appeared to be watching her sitting at the wheel of the van, she didn't think twice about it at the time. It was not uncommon for men to stare at her. If only she had been more alert—more aware of her surroundings, she wouldn't be in this mess right now. She had always thought of herself as being pretty observant, but this had certainly shot holes in that theory. All the signs had been there, from seeing him at the book signings to seeing him in the van and being too blind to put two and two together. Maybe she deserved this, she thought wryly.

Her thoughts drifted to Edward. He had probably been worried sick. She wished there were some way she could let him know she was alive, but without a phone or computer, the only way she could do that was to get free. Her eyes once again scanned the interior of the Winnebago and came to rest on the handle of the scissors. In his clearing out of the utensils and other possible weaponry, apparently, this had still been forgotten. A hint of a smile played across her lips briefly as she continued typing. She had at least one weapon she could count on and she intended to use it at the opportune time. The only other weapon that was accessible to her were the very gifts that she typed with now, her hands. Removing them from the keys and turning them palm up, she clenched them into tight fists. In her mind, she threw a rapid succession of upper cuts and strong, karate punches. *Makuso*, she whispered and her breathing deepened, her pulse slowed. Her mind and body became one. Although she knew her sense of time was off, she knew she must have been in captivity for at least a week, maybe longer. She tried counting every nightfall and sunrise. The last newspaper she remembered seeing was five to six days ago. After remaining in one place for so long, what had caused him to flee, she wondered. Were the police closing in? Her heart soared at the possibility, but was quickly grounded as she thought about the police finding her lifeless body somewhere.

Mia noticed that Parker seemed more confused than when he first abducted her. He constantly went back and forth between calling her Mia and Valerie, his grasp on reality continuing to slip away from him. She knew that he honestly believed they were two separate people. Having never been in the company of someone who suffered from this type of dementia, his fluctuating behavior always left her with an icy, cold fear that remained with her for the day or until his next episode. But, she was thankful that there had been no cigarette burn incidents in days. She did exactly as she was told and typed for as many hours as she could during the day. Amazingly, she was almost half way through the story, surprised at how much she had been able to recall. Parker hadn't bothered to read any of it, yet. That too, surprised her. However, he would be the one surprised to see that the victim, his beloved Valerie Lassiter, would become the victor. That was also her plan and promise to herself.

"I don't hear any typing back there," Parker yelled from the front of the vehicle. "What are you two up to?" he continued.

Mia rolled her eyes in disgust, all too familiar with these episodes, "I'm sorry, I was just stretching my fingers," she replied, picking up her rhythm again on the sticking keys.

"You're such a slacker, nothing like Valerie."

Mia cleared her throat, thinking that it might be better not to speak, but deciding against it. "If my hands were free, I could type a lot faster," she spoke haltingly.

"Free?" he asked incredulously. "We're not there yet."

"Well, where are we—where are we going?" Mia interrupted.

"You'll see when we get there. And please don't interrupt me again," Parker admonished. "At the first opportunity, you would try to turn Valerie against me and I won't have that. Oh yeah and if you were thinking of using these," Parker held up a shiny pair of stainless steel scissors. "Then just think again."

Mia's hands fell from the keys and her mouth went dry. Her plan had been thwarted. She looked at the stack of newspapers. Sure enough, the scissors were gone. *When did he get them?* her mind raced. She thought for a moment.

"I don't know what you're talking about, Parker."

"Maybe you don't Val, but Mia certainly does," he hissed.

"Parker, where are we going?" Mia pleaded.

Many times when he referred to her and Valerie as two different people, she thought to play along, but was unsure of what the outcome might be. This time she didn't care.

"I would never let Mia do that—never. She knows you care deeply for me, as I do for you."
Parker's heart pounded in his chest so violently, he had trouble holding on to the steering wheel. Fortunately, he was just approaching the next rest stop and swerved recklessly on to the shoulder, bringing the camper and van to a screeching halt. He could hardly believe what he was hearing. Could it be true? Someone finally cared about him. Sure, he knew that Valerie would be a part of his future, but he always assumed that he would have to force her to reciprocate those feelings. Awestruck, he searched for a response. He didn't want Mia involved in this conversation any more than was required. Not turning to face Mia, he spoke to the rear-view mirror, only his eyes visible as he gauged her expressions.

"If she cares for me the way you say, then why is she allowing you to run her life and dictate this relationship—why isn't she fighting?" he inquired.

Mia spoke to the back of his head, but looked him directly in the eyes, gauging his expression as well, "I am fighting—fighting for us. But, I need more control...Parker."
Parker gasped. He could not believe his eyes or his ears as he turned to face her.

"How?—Valerie, it's really you."

"Of course it's me. How could you have ever doubted that I was here for you."
Parker placed the gear in park and approached her with tears in his eyes as he knelt and stared—straight through Mia. Mia removed her hands from the typewriter keys and held his gaze. He lifted one pale, thin hand and smoothed back a wayward strand of hair so that it lay among the rest of her

matted mass. He seemed hypnotized and almost childlike in his appearance. If she played her cards right, pretending to be Valerie could work in her favor. The thought to play this out had never occurred to her because she had been too afraid. However, nothing could have prepared her for his reaction as he laid his head in her lap and whispered, "Mother."

Chapter Fourteen

The predominately deserted trailer park was in an area that Edward never knew existed. The winding, dirt path continued uphill and revealed tall, patches of wild grass which partially concealed four motorhomes. He eased the Jaguar past four run down trailers, comparing the numbers on the mailboxes to those on the piece of paper in his hand. The homes were spaced approximately 120 yards or more apart. Frustrated, Edward circled back around, weaving in, out and around rusted, abandoned vehicles, discarded garbage bins and broken furniture. Plumes of dust were left in his wake as he slammed on his brakes and made an abrupt stop. Looking around, he discovered that this secluded area seemed to be some sort of hideaway for misfits of society. He squinted, trying to see if anyone would peek out of their windows or open their doors to see what was going on—no one did.

Edward sat for a long while, the 8-cylinder engine of the Jaguar idling smoothly. He looked at the address on the piece of paper again, 98 Desert Lane. Studying the sequence of numbers and comparing them to the ones on the mailbox he was closest to, 90 Desert Lane appeared to be valid. He placed the car in drive and continued along the dirt path. Upon closer inspection, he noticed that each motorhome was equally deteriorated. However, some had been exposed to its owner's personal touches; a door hanging off its hinges, a window broken and one home entirely supported by milk crates. Graffiti adorned the left side of two of the homes and mountains of garbage had been piled along the side of another. The more Edward observed, the more he began to realize that this neighborhood, such as it was, didn't look like a legitimate trailer park community. Nor, did it look like a pit stop for motor homes, but rather a piece of land that had been inhabited by a few people who didn't believe in paying taxes or any other expenses incurred with living in a normal society. He wondered if the land had undergone all of the proper zoning procedures and irrigation measures to qualify it as a legal City and County road. Edward continued along the road for a short time and stopped again near an area of open space with a row of four mailboxes. The space where a motorhome should be was empty, but according to his calculations, this spot would be 98 Desert Road.

Edward unfastened his seat belt and quickly exited the vehicle. He walked up to the mailbox and noticed the black, adhesive letters had been removed, but the outline clearly revealed the numbers 98. His heart began to hammer in his chest. He was so close, yet so far from finding his wife that it made his blood run cold. He turned, taking in a complete view of the area. Ironically, the vantagepoint from where he stood, which would have been where the motorhome was, had a beautiful view of most of the Los Angeles area. Standing on top of this hill looking down on the busy, crowded city, Edward was reminded of a place called 'Kissing Canyon' where the teenage boys used to take their girlfriends when he was in high school. "Where are you, Mia," he whispered to himself as he squeezed his eyes shut, to keep from screaming in frustration. He knew he was close—that this was the place where his wife had been. He *knew* it was the right place.

He re-entered his vehicle and backed up to the last home in the row of four. As he exited the vehicle and approached the front of the motorhome, he noticed movement in one of the open windows, but couldn't figure out if the form was male or female. He knocked on the door, but received no answer and quickly knocked again. Soon, the knock was answered by a haggard looking woman with dirty-blond, hair. Her large frame filled the doorway as she stood with one hand on her hip, as if she'd been expecting him. A dirty apron covered the flowered print housedress and her feet were shoved into filthy animal slippers.

"Yeah?"

Edward looked up into her pock-marked face and cleared his throat, "Um, excuse me ma'am. I was wondering if you have seen either of these people around here recently?" Edward removed the folded picture of Parker from the breast pocket of his jacket and then retrieved one of Mia from his wallet. The lady reluctantly took them both and examined them quickly. She then handed the pictures back and craned her neck to get a better view of the Jaguar parked in front of her door.

"You a cop?"

"No, I assure you I'm not a cop," Edward said with mild frustration.

"Then what do you want with these folks?"

"Well, I'm looking for my wife and I believe this man knows where she is."

The lady paused for a moment, "You know, just 'cause we live in trailers and can't afford to drive no fancy cars don't make you people that live down there no better than us," she said gesturing to the view of Los Angeles that Edward had just observed.

"I understand and respect that ma'am, I never had anything fall in my lap either, and right now I'm going through a time so bad that I would gladly trade places with you if I thought it would bring my wife back."

"Well I guess you ain't been 'round a lot of poor folks in your life," she said staring Edward straight in the eyes. "Let me see them pictures again." She observed them closely this time, taking particular notice of the picture of Mia than of Parker. "Well, I'm sure you know that whatever this fella's name is don up and gone. Left here yesterday mid-mornin'. Figured he was on the run for something. When folks leave from here that's usually the case."

"So, do you know this man, Parker McKinley?"

"Know 'em by face, but that's it. See, 'round here,

we don't bother with names, because it's not important. And, it's just plain dangerous. The less you know 'bout a person, the better off you is. But now, the woman, your wife, I can't say I have seen her."

"Exactly what does that mean?"

"It means about a week ago, late in the night, I had come out to throw out the trash. 'Cause 'ya see it's better to do it late at night so won't nobody see 'ya..."

"Yeah, I understand, but what did you see?"

"Oh, yeah. Well, I'm out here throwin' out the trash, when I sees that fella's van pull up. And of course, there wasn't nothin' odd or strange 'bout that,——"

"You mean a van or his motorhome?"

"I mean his van. See, he's got some ratty, old van he drives around, as well as the motorhome, which ain't in no better condition than mines here."

"Okay."

"So, after he gets out the van, he looks 'round before openin' up the back doors, then carries something out the back."

"What was it?" Edward asked, his heart quickening its pace.

"Now can't say I seen what it was or seen it movin'. If it was a person, he or she mighta been drunk or doped up on somethin' though. But anyhow, he struggled with it to get it inside 'cause he's a little fella 'ya know and that was all I seen."

"Does he have company often?"

"Nope. I don't think so, but I don't always see him comin' and goin'. But I see him come in sometimes with grocery bags and them little white prescription bags."

"Did he see you when all of this was going on?"

"I don't think so. In fact I hope not, especially if people are lookin' for him. It's an unspoken code up here that we don't talk to no cops. And, it wasn't like I could just pick up the phone and call one if I wanted to anyhow. But, everybody up here minds their own business—except me, I try to help where I can," she said giggling. "I don't say nothin' to no one and they don't say nothin' to me, but my eyes are always open,"she continued.

"And you didn't see a lady with him yesterday morning when he left?"

"No. But, anyone coulda been in the trailer. I don't know."

"You've been very helpful."
Edward pulled out his wallet and extracted a crisp one hundred-dollar bill. He handed it to the lady and thanked her.

"You are soooooo welcome mister," the lady said to his retreating footsteps as she quickly shut her door.
Edward paused at his car door. He removed the address from his pants pocket and balled up the piece of paper in his hand. Although he dropped it in the dirt and let the wind carry it away, his heart soared with renewed optimism that Mia was alive, but he didn't know for how much longer. He began dialing Sergeant Williams' number from his car phone to fill him in on the recent developments.

There was a time when she could pick up the phone and discuss her feelings with her best friend. But after the past week, she didn't think she would ever get that opportunity again. In her heart, she had already started the mourning process, and in some ways had started trying to get on with her life. She was extremely ashamed of what she had attempted with Edward. It was like she wasn't herself. Sure, there were many times when she had been lonely and envied Mia's life and her marriage, but not to the extent of trying to seduce her husband, or so she thought. Maybe because Michael had shown her that someone could be interested in just her, was she now able to rationalize this situation. It was funny how things worked. For the entire time she had known Mia she wished she could be her—trade places with her for just a while. However, today, she wouldn't want to trade places for anything in the world.

Lynda walked through the front door of her town-house and flopped down on the leather loveseat. The phone began ringing and she started to answer it but decided she didn't feel like talking right now. She knew it couldn't be Michael calling her that soon. Only two minutes ago had she stepped out of his BMW. She listened to the voice as the machine began to record. "Hi Lynda, it's me. If you're there pick up." There was a short pause. "Oh well, guess not. Just calling to see how the date went. Call me tomorrow with *all* the details."

Her sister, Gayle. She knew it would be her. "I'm glad I followed my first mind and didn't answer the phone," she said aloud. She loved her big sister, but she had less of a life than Lynda. And, as a result, she lived for any details from dates that Lynda could provide her, which hadn't been much lately.

Lynda removed her pumps and padded to the bath-room in her stockinged feet. She ran a warm bath and poured lilac scented oil into the stream of running water, watching as thousands of tiny bubbles appeared before her eyes.

Anxious to envelop herself in the warm water, she removed her wraparound dress and stockings and threw them in a pile just outside the bathroom door. As she immersed herself in the soothing water, she shut off the brass fixtures to stop the flow and released a sigh. She lay back enjoying the aromatherapy of the oil as the scent wafted up around her, relaxing her tight, tense muscles. Focusing in on the music that played softly in the background, *A House Is Not A Home*, she chimed in singing barely above a whisper. "I climb the stairs and turn the key. Oh please be there..."

Her thoughts floated to her evening with Michael and she could feel a heat radiating from her center that had nothing to do with the warm bath water. This had been their third date in the past week and Lynda had really started looking forward to seeing him each time. Whenever she saw him, she was left breathless by his very essence. The way he carried himself with his strong, smooth, chiseled features, mocha-colored face and startling white teeth were enough to turn her to butter. His captivating demeanor when he discussed the specifics of his job as an architect and the fact that he was in the process of designing a building for a brand new software company in New York, left Lynda in awe. He had been gracious enough to show her the plans and from the looks of it, it was going to be a spectacular work of art. From the hexagonal glass design to the helicopter landing pad on the top.

But, as swept away as she was, she promised herself that her next relationship would be taken very slowly. They had not yet slept together, but it had nothing to do with the lack of desire on either part. In fact, she knew that if they didn't do something soon he would probably start to think she was some sort of tease or something. There had been plenty of close calls, but she wanted to make sure that he was in this for longer than just a roll in the hay. She had explained this to him and felt that he understood, but whenever they had these close calls, his furrowed brow quickly turned to a look of understanding and acceptance. He assured her that he understood liking a person and wanting to make sure that they liked you for you and not because of the way you looked or your occupation. Lynda assumed that he too, had been scorned at least once before by someone that had been more infatuated by his occupation and looks than who he really was. A single, available architect, you just didn't see that everyday—and she had to admit that it had certainly re-fueled those heated embers in her to learn that she was involved with one.

Almost instinctively she reached for the phone she had placed on the floor near the tub. Her thoughts returned to Mia. Normally, she would have called her after every date and given her all the details. A wave of sadness washed over her. She very well may never have that opportunity again.

Her sorrow deepened and for the first time since her friend had been missing, she cried like baby.

Chapter Fifteen

Mia and Valerie had become one. Mia answered to the name of Valerie and played along, catering to her captor's fantasy when required. In fact, she played the role so convincingly, that she was beginning to question her own sanity. The past couple of days had been a real test in mind control. After arriving in San Francisco, they had driven around, "Taking in the sights," as Parker had phrased it. He made his own rest stops, pulling over on residential streets or in vacant parking lots, but moving on before the police could come by and issue a citation. During one close call, when they were parked in the lot of a 7-11 convenience store, a police officer, seemed to come out of nowhere. He had obviously been watching the van for some time and decided to inquire as to why the van had been sitting there for so long. Mia was chained in her usual position on the fold out chair, when the tap on the driver's side window brought her fully alert. Only moments before, Parker turned to her with a look in his eyes that she had never seen before. It was mixed with desperation, fear of loss and total madness. She looked at him and then down at the shiny, .38 pistol that he held in his left hand.

"Don't even think about breathing a word," he hissed.

Mia's eyes were wide with terror, she swallowed hard and obeyed. She never knew he had a weapon, but then maybe the opportunity never arose for him to show her one—before now. She watched as Parker calmly, held her at gunpoint with his left hand and conversed and passed his license to the officer with his right. She wanted to scream, holler and kick—let the officer know that she was there and desperately wanted to go home. She wanted to ask him why wasn't he checking this person's registration and running his license plates through DMV. Wasn't anybody looking for her? Did the hunt for her begin and end in Los Angeles? Instead, she squeezed her eyes shut and bit her lip to keep from screaming as a steady stream of tears drenched her face.

"That's my Valerie," he said as they pulled into traffic and headed for the highway.

After two days in San Francisco, they arrived early morning in Las Vegas. Parker shared his thoughts with Valerie of wanting to stay there for a long time. He loved the wide, open spaces and the deserted atmosphere. He said it made him feel free as he chastised his mother for never being the mother she should have been and cursed Mia for her bad influence on Valerie.

As Parker's symptoms became progressively worse, Mia had not progressed any further on her manuscript than she had a few days ago, because as Valerie, she didn't have to do that kind of work. However, between Parker's psychotic episodes, it was hard for Mia to continue at this pace. Today, she could be Mia, Valerie or his mother, it all depended on who he felt like interacting with.

Mia and Valerie were close to gaining Parker's complete trust. He actually let them free this morning with the promise of blowing their brains out if they tried to leave him. As they walked along the perimeter of the Grand Canyon, Mia contemplated several scenarios in her head, all of which concluded with her captor's demise. The reality, however, was that he had a gun aimed at her the entire time as they walked calmly along the rocky terrain. Odds were good that she was the one who would wind up dead.

As dusk settled on the desert, the burnt-orange sun dipped behind the mountains, playing peek-a-boo between the peaks and valleys. Mia knew that her time was fast approaching to escape. She had garnered the long-awaited trust of being shackle-free around him, but now there was the issue of the gun. As she walked along with Parker, listening to him drone on to Valerie about his plans for their future, she wondered what it would feel like to be shot.

Would it hurt? Would she be paralyzed? Or would she simply die? The reality was that it was a risk she had to take or die a mental death at the hands of her abductor, Parker McKinley.

Mia had never given much thought as to how she would die, except that she expected to be old when it happened. One thing she had decided throughout this trek, was that she was going out fighting. She had been a fighter all her life, always having to prove her whiteness or blackness because of her fair skin and naturally wavy hair. When she got older, she grew tired of explaining to people that she was in fact Black. That both her mother and father were Creole and that made her just as black as any other Black person. In her current situation, she wondered if her skin had been darker would this be happening to her. Did Parker think she was White? More importantly did he care? She figured that it was of little concern to him. For what he found, or so he thought, was a soul mate—someone who identified with him and understood his plight. However, what he failed to understand was that if he had to hold a gun on her, then they obviously didn't see eye to eye, least of all were they soul mates.

"Valerie, my sweet. What do you think of spending the rest of our lives here? It's such a great place to live and die," Parker marveled, encroaching into Mia's thoughts.

"You know death has never really been something I've thought about until this very moment." As he reflected on his life, he thought about how he had spent his time on this planet. "It doesn't matter much to me—Heaven, Hell, I don't believe in either one so what's the point in being a good person. However, if there is a Hell, I'm quite sure I've been in it for all of my life," Parker said waving his pistol.

"I'm sure you've had some good times in your life," Mia lied.

"My sweet, Val. Between being in and out of institutions, psychiatrist offices and living in seclusion, I really haven't had much of a life at all in all my years of living. As my mother told me so many times when I was younger, I'm a failure," Parker looked away sadly. For a moment, Mia actually felt bad for him. He had tried to capture love and add some sense of normalcy to his otherwise empty life and had certainly failed miserably at it. Maybe death was the one thing he could be successful at. But she had no sympathy for his methods of trying to establish that normalcy.

Mia mentally got into character as Valerie. "I think living here would be great. But, I really wish you would trust me enough to stop pointing that thing at me."

Parker shook his head this time, uncertainty written across his face. Mia swore she saw his grip loosen on the pistol, but for just a moment and then he quickly recovered. "Can't you understand Val, the control that Mia has over you? I can't risk her doing something stupid. It would ruin everything. I just can't."

"I understand. How long then do you think she will have this control over me?" Mia pried.

"It's really hard to say. I see her when I see you, yet I see *only* her in your eyes."

Mia thought she noticed a glimpse of genuine remorse in his face, but couldn't be sure. Apparently, he wanted to see genuine sincerity in her eyes, she thought blowing out an exasperated breath. This was something she wasn't sure she would be able to pull off. Basically, she had to act as much in love with him as he was with Valerie. They walked along a little path that spiraled down between two huge boulders, in silence. As Parker admired the rich, adobe-colored, rock formations, Mia plotted her escape.

"You know Parker, this place is so beautiful. I could really see us living here for the rest of our lives." Parker stopped dead in his tracks.

"Valerie, do you mean that?"

"Of course I do and I know you feel the same way. We get along so wonderfully and this place is so special.

I've never seen it before 'ya know."

"Yes, I know. I know. You see we have something special, Valerie. You could never imagine." He walked closer to her until they were face-to-face. She could smell the sourness of his breath. He bent his knees just slightly to stare directly into her eyes. Mia knew he was looking through her to Valerie—looking for the sincerity and love that he longed for. Trying her best to numb her feelings and look at him as if he were Edward, her loving husband, Mia's eyes softened. From them, radiated an expression of love that had never been shown to Parker McKinley in his entire life. Seeing the sudden realization in Parker's eyes, for effect, she added, "I love you, Parker."

Suddenly, he raised the gun above his head and into the air and began shooting. Mia crouched where she was standing and placed her arms protectively over her head. He shot the gun five or six times, Mia couldn't be sure. She didn't know much about guns—in fact she knew nothing, but she knew that most handguns possessed the capability to hold six bullets and possibly one in the chamber.

"Did you hear that mother? She loves me. Someone is finally willing to return my feelings and do what *you* didn't all those years—I hope you rot in Hell. She *really* loves me," he screamed at the top of his lungs. The sound encompassed Mia and reverberated throughout her brain. She stood back up to face him, nervous and wobbly from the barrage of gunfire and managed a smile.

"So we don't have to worry about Mia any more. I have complete control over the situation, thanks to you. And, I have made sure she won't be back anymore," Mia said convincingly.

Parker smiled and Mia was sure it was the first time she had seen that happen. He threw the gun as far and as hard as he could and it whistled in the air. When it landed, a bullet discharged and seemed to ricochet from every angle. Mia threw herself on the ground again, but Parker remained standing, as if oblivious to anything that was going on. When she stood, the realization hit her that the dynamics of this game had changed.

Finally, she thought. She knew the odds were far from even, but at least now she had a fighting chance to get out of this mess. To her knowledge, there were no more weapons around, except for the can of disinfectant spray she planned to use as mace, but that was in the camper. The big question now was, when? When would she make her move? An onslaught of unexpected rain brought Mia out of her reverie.

"Well, it's dark and starting to rain, Val. I think we should head home. God, how I love the sound of that. Home."

Mia cringed at his words. Not only had he taken to calling her a fictional character from a book, but he had become so comfortable with it that he even abbreviated the name to a pet name. She complied, "So do I."

Too quickly for Mia, they reached the motorhome. Her mouth went dry and her heart began to beat so loud she thought Parker would hear it. He opened the door for her and she quickly noted the sudden consciousness of manners he had acquired. She used the door to support her weight as she took a huge step up and into the motorhome while Parker brought up the rear. Once inside, she took a seat on the foldout cot, suddenly feeling more awkward than ever before, the constant companionship of the shackles and ropes no longer there to keep her company. Deciding to test the waters, Mia stood to see how far her comfort level would be tolerated.

"Why don't I make us some dinner, to celebrate?" she offered nervously.

"That's a great idea. I'll just lay over here and take a little nap. I'm awfully tired."

This was too easy, Mia thought. She was suspicious, but he *had* thrown the gun away. The thought clung to her like wet clothing. If she had tried this days ago, maybe all of this would be behind her now. But, she was still suspicious. She stooped down to retrieve two frozen dinners from the mini-refrigerator and decided to sneak a peak at the can of disinfectant spray. It was still there. Returning her focus back to the frozen dinners, she chose Salisbury steak and chicken fettucini platters. Just as she closed the refrigerator door and stood to place the meals on the counter, she felt hands around her neck. Suddenly, she couldn't breath—couldn't think, but in the midst of this, she had a perfect moment of clarity. She knew exactly what was happening—her plan had not gone as smoothly as she thought. Mia flailed and thrashed about, but went rigid when the six-inch blade was waved in front of her face.

"Do you think I'm stupid? Valerie is not in control, it's still you. But I'm going to see to it that you don't bother us anymore," Parker spoke harshly into her ear.

"Our Father, who art in Heaven—" Mia began, knowing that her end was now and hoping that there would be no pain.

Chapter Sixteen

The day was unusually cool, despite the fact that summer had officially arrived. People were clad in sweaters and jeans instead of shorts and tank tops and they seemed to move a little faster than usual. Everywhere you looked there were red, white and blue decorations and flags signifying up-coming parades and the Fourth of July Holiday. Department stores displayed televisions for sale and previewed vacation trips and family specials that portrayed family and friends sitting around picnic tables in preparation for Independence Day.

Edward maneuvered the Jaguar through the evening traffic almost oblivious that his mother was in the car with him. He had taken her on a shopping spree in celebration of her birthday. Every year she visited for a week and they would browse around the boutiques and shops on Rodeo Drive. Edward paid for the first-class, round trip ticket because he knew his mother and father could not afford it on their fixed-incomes. Normally, on their shopping excursions they would stop in exquisite, little coffeehouses, bakeries and candy shops, but this time Edward just didn't have it in him.

The stress and anguish had become just too much for him. However, he put on his bravest front and smiled at the appropriate times, masking the pain that plagued him. It had worked so far, or so he thought.

"Maybe we shouldn't have gone shopping this time, son. I know your heart isn't in it and of course, I totally understand. After all, it is your wedding anniversary."

"No mom. This is really just what I needed—to give my mind a rest. I realize that no matter how painful, I have to continue to be strong. My wife is missing and I am helpless to do anything about it. I just hope we can find her before it's too late."

Dorothy Simone took an aged-spotted, wrinkled hand and placed it firmly on her son's shoulder. "I know how much you love her. We all do. I really believe she's okay and trying desperately to get back to you. All we can do is pray."

Edward continued to weave his way through traffic until he reached the expressway heading toward LAX. He and his mother drove for several miles in mutual silence. The visit had gone by quickly and she was flying out today. Although he was always sad when she left, Edward was almost sorry he had agreed to her visit this year because he knew he had been lousy company. It was important to him to convey a strong image to his mother, but she had always been able to see right through him.

As they approached the short-term parking garage, Edward was hit with a wave of panic so fierce, he had to pull the car over to catch his breath.

"Edward, are you okay?" his mother asked with obvious concern.

Edward took a few moments before answering. "This is where it all happened, mom. This is where the police believe Mia disappeared."

"Oh, baby. I'm so sorry," she said reaching awkwardly over the seatbelt to hug her son. For the first time since Mia's disappearance, Edward cried. His mother hugged him and he somehow drew from her strength because at this moment, he didn't have to be strong. He allowed himself to be purged of all the emotions he had been feeling since his wife had been gone. The emotions of guilt, anger, anxiety and hurt were gone now. In their place, however, was a profound loneliness that left him as hollow as a shell, but he was much stronger since his visit to the trailer park. He was hopeful that his wife would be found before it was too late.

Edward decided to touch base with Sergeant

Williams at the police department. They had not spoken in over three days. The sergeant was good about keeping him abreast of any significant developments, so he was fairly certain that nothing had developed since they last spoke. *But just in case*, he thought. He approached the guard's desk and was greeted by none other than Officer Ross —the same officer that helped him when he first came into the precinct early last week. Despite their obvious dislike for one another, they had learned to be civil.

"Good afternoon, Officer Ross. Is Sergeant Williams on duty today?"

"Mr. Simone. He is. He has someone in his office right now, though. Should be finishing up soon?"

"Great. I'll just take a seat over here and wait."

Edward took a seat on the hard, wooden bench in the waiting area debating whether or not to tell Sergeant Williams *all* about his self-conducted investigation at the trailer park where Parker McKinley lived. He figured they already knew Parker was no longer there and if they had bothered to ask around, knew that he was on the run. Within moments, Sergeant Williams appeared from behind the closed door with a middle-aged couple. From the bits of conversation Edward picked up, apparently, their son or daughter had been missing since yesterday after school. Edward couldn't help but become more interested and sympathetic as the mother stood crying hysterically. Sergeant Williams offered comforting words and a reassuring smile just as he had done for Edward. The man, trying hard to be strong, supportively placed his arm around his wife's waist as they left the station.

Edward approached the burly sergeant. They exchanged a hearty handshake as they took their usual seats in Sergeant William's office.

"Another missing person, huh?" Edward asked solemnly.

"Unfortunately, yes. More specifically a child."

He blew out an exasperated breath. "But, you have enough to worry about."

"You're right. I just wanted to touch base with you as to any new developments."

"Not much to report since last time we spoke, really. As you know, through the Department of Motor Vehicles, we were able to track down what we thought was a current address."

"But?" Edward asked, already knowing the answer.

"It was predominately abandoned. A mailbox with the outline of an address was there, but no trailer, van or anything. For all practical intents and purposes, he's on the lambe."

"Did you talk to anyone up there. See if they'd seen anything or possibly knew him?" Edward asked, knowing the police had received little or no cooperation with the folks on that secluded, dirt road.

"No. However, not for lack of trying. According to one of my officers, they attempted to knock on the four remaining motorhomes, but no one answered their door. It's not uncommon for people like that to stick together. Obviously, this is not a legal trailer park community, but more of a place that these people have chosen to inhabit. I guess in this case, it was good that you went there first and was actually able to speak to someone. Although, I don't condone civilians playing cop."

Edward was stunned. "How'd you know," Edward asked guiltily. "I just—"

"Hey, no need to explain, I didn't say I didn't understand it—in some situations. Certainly, this would be one and I know what I'd do if it were my wife."

Edward breathed a sigh of relief. "I just felt I needed to do more, 'ya know what I mean?"

"Yes, I do," Sergeant Williams responded knowingly.

"So, where do you think my wife is now? Where

would he most likely go? Have you located any family or friends that he might be hiding with?"

"We're checking on all his affiliations now. Although we don't think we're going to find any. He is a loner in the truest sense of the word. One good thing is that we think we have a pretty good description of the motorhome. That's certainly a plus. We've received a few calls from people saying they've spotted a motorhome with a van in tow. It seems to fit the description we have now. As for where he's headed and if Mia's with him, the last sighting was off the major highway heading toward Nevada."

"What do you mean *if* Mia's with him?" Edward asked defensively.

"Edward it's like I said before, right now we just want to talk to this guy. Even though we were unable to lift his prints from Mia's vehicle, we have him on auto theft given the identification by the garage attendant. Yet, we still have no hard proof that he has Mia."

"Look Sergeant, no disrespect, but does my wife have to be discovered a month from now in some shallow grave in order for you guys to start treating him like a dangerous suspect?"

Sergeant Williams' facial expression never changed. He began calmly, "He is a suspect in this case, the only one we have at the moment, but it still doesn't mean he has committed a crime. All we have is circumstantial evidence. And, you must remember, you were a suspect in the case first, but it doesn't mean anything without hard evidence."

Edward sat back in his seat, "You've made your point," he said feeling offended.

"I just need to make sure you understand the process."

"Yeah, I think I'm beginning to."

"Well, we also had a sighting on Highway 101 near San Francisco. He's covered a lot of ground over the past few days apparently."

"Does he know someone in Nevada?" Edward asked trying to take the tension out of his voice.

"We don't know yet. My guess is that he doesn't. From the information Dr. Fischer was able to provide us from his medical records, he has no living relatives to speak of."

"Then why Nevada?"

"I don't know. But for that matter why anywhere? Why resort to kidnapping someone? And, why your wife, of all the authors in the world? Edward, these are questions we will probably never know the answers to. Especially since we're not psychologists. But, I do think we are closer now than ever before. The 'all points bulletin' and the reward money are real incentives, but then you have some people that just really try to be good citizens by reporting anything they see that seems suspicious. Those are the folks we are relying on."

Edward rose to leave, "Thank you Sergeant. I really appreciate you tolerating my drop-ins and giving this case so much of your time."

"Don't mention it. I try to give all my cases priority, I really do. And, as I said we're close."

Edward opened the door and then paused. He turned to face the sergeant and bit down on his lip as if uncertain. "Just one last question?"

"Sure."

"You said you believe we're close."

"Yes. I do."

"But, close to what? If and when this psycho is found, will Mia even be with him? Will my wife be alive?"

Sergeant Williams looked away and for the first time in their numerous meetings, he didn't look Edward in the eyes. "I wish I could tell you what you want to hear, but I simply don't have the answer to that."

"Yeah, I know." Edward turned and closed the

door softly behind him.

Lynda slammed the phone down in its cradle. *Humph. Who the hell does he think he is*, she thought bitterly. This was the fourth time in two days that she had tried to contact Edward and he had not returned her calls. Obviously, he was screening his calls at home and at work. She had even gone so far as to get his work number from information, thinking that she could reach him there, but had been blocked by his very obedient secretary. Why was he avoiding her? She had apologized for her behavior and he had made it clear that the entire scene was a mistake. But, he had told her that he would call if there was anything he felt she should know about the case. Surely something had developed by now even though nothing had appeared in the news recently. No matter what happened, she and Mia would always be friends, so what made him think she didn't have a right to know what was happening. Normally, she would storm right over to the house, but she was afraid it would be a wasted trip. She knew she had burned her bridges with Edward, but she couldn't live with herself if she didn't at least try to make it right. Her heart grew heavy knowing that she would probably never see her best friend again. Sure, Mia was a fighter, but statistics showed that the longer a person was missing, the more likely it was that they would be found dead. Lynda fought back the stinging sensation in the corner of her eyes. She would make sure to wipe the slate clean with her best friend's husband. It was the least she could do.

Lynda cleared off her desk and placed a few files in her tote bag. Not that she thought the opportunity would arise that she would be doing any work this weekend, but just in case. She synchronized her PalmPilot and dropped that in her bag too. There were two authors she was trying to get to appear at the store next month and she might need to try and catch their publicists at home. Butterfly flurries tickled her stomach and she smiled like a schoolgirl at the thought of her upcoming weekend. The time had finally arrived. She and Michael were staying the weekend at the upscale Beverly Hills Hotel. Although they had been to each other's house before, they both agreed that a neutral location for their first time together, would add to the intimacy of the experience.

She leaned back in her swivel chair thinking about the night and days to come. It had been a long time since she had been intimate with someone, but it had been even longer since she had been willing to take a risk and give of her heart. The truth was, she was excited and unaware of how much she had been missing. Receiving flowers, going to jazz clubs and attending movies had rekindled an all but forgotten part of her. She closed her eyes and could still feel the warmth and tenderness of their last kiss. Michael hadn't rushed her. In fact, she would have given in long ago, but it was Michael who had insisted on doing things right. She smiled in spite of her self. Maybe she had finally found a man who could measure up to the great Edward Simone. Maybe, she could finally extinguish the torch she had been carrying for her best friend's husband all these years. As she hefted the tote onto her shoulder, she took one last look around her office to make sure she wasn't forgetting anything. "After tonight, I might be able to write a book myself," she said aloud as she switched off the desk lamp and strolled out of her office.

Chapter Seventeen

The gleam from the blade reflected brightly in the corner of Mia's eye. She had made her peace, but she was not ready to die—not this way and not without a fight. The knife seemed to have a will of its own as it pressed harder and harder into the tender flesh of her neck. She angled her head to the left and slightly away from the sharpest point of the knife, but it followed her, as did Parker's one-armed grip around her shoulders.

Mia could feel the spray of spittle on the side of her face as Parker vehemently promised to rid her of Valerie's body. Her mind raced frantically to figure out what she could say to buy some time.

"What about the manuscript?" she managed. "How will you ever know if Valerie lives?"

Parker's grasp loosened, but remained forceful. Mia felt a trickle of something wet land on her hand and was alarmed to see that it was blood, her own she could only assume. She gasped.

"Don't get cute with me. You think you're so smart. I know Valerie lives, unfortunately it's in you, but I plan to change all that."

"Okay, okay. But, don't you understand that if you kill me, you kill Valerie, too?"

Parker loosened his grip even more and Mia knew it was now or never. As soon as she felt the blade pull slightly away from her neck, she was thrust years back to the confident teenager going up for her purple belt in the Karate promotional. She quickly stepped back, bracing her right leg between Parker's. With her right arm in a rising block position between her neck and his hand, Parker fiercely held on to the knife.

She could hear him gasp in surprise and knew that Parker had been caught completely off guard. A quick elbow to the ribs hurled her attacker back a few feet, yet he maintained his grip on the knife. His grip on the knife was relentless.

"You bitch," he hissed.

Mia's breath came in ragged gasps. Before Parker could recover, she aimed for his groin, but landed a firm, front kick - *Fumikomi*, in his lower stomach, which doubled him over.

"Kyu," Mia screamed, as a seasoned martial arts student would at the end of a successful move. She grabbed the foldout chair and brought it down hard on Parker's arm and hand. The knife finally dropped to the floor as Parker squealed in pain.

Instinctively, he lunged forward, the weight of his body forcing Mia back and off her feet. She slammed down hard on the floor, but not before hitting her head on the table in the process. Fighting fervently for consciousness, she struggled to get out from under Parker's weight. She knew if he overpowered her, this time, it was over. He managed to gain the upper hand and lock one of her arms near her side and between his legs as he fought to gain control of the other one. Mia could feel her strength and endurance diminishing as she squirmed to get him off of her while flailing wildly with her free hand. She moved her head frantically from side to side and noticed that she was at eye level with the shiny spray can she had seen so many times. Reaching her hand as far above her head as she could, she only succeeded in hearing her nails scrape the can.

Parker had been mumbling something that Mia could not make out. It had become a mantra that had been added to the various background noises of her ragged breathing and scuffle to get free. However, he was tiring of the games and wrapped both hands around her neck. Mia's mouth worked, but produced no sound. Darkness crept in at the corners of her vision as Parker leaned in closer to her, applying more force around her throat.

"Die, die, die," Parker repeated.

Mia dug her heels into the ground and managed to scoot herself and Parker upwards in excess of an inch. Her free hand reached up and out toward the spray can, only this time with success.

Parker leaned in even closer to Mia's face, as if wanting to see the light of life extinguished from her eyes. She closed her eyes and maneuvered the can between their faces, spraying a steady stream into Parker's eyes. He howled like a wounded animal and toppled off of her onto the floor. Mia gulped in as much air as she could while pulling herself up to make it to the door. Freedom was in sight. However, just as she placed her hand on the knob and opened the door to descend the two small steps, she felt a vice-like grip on her ankle that brought her down hard again on the floor of the motorhome.

"No," she cried kicking and flailing.

Parker managed to bring them both up on their feet as he held both of Mia's arms close to her side. They stood facing one another, breathing heavily.

"You betrayed me Valerie. You're just as bad as she is," Parker said with tears in his eyes. "I thought you loved me. I thought you were in control" he continued. "I'm sorry, I'm so sorry."

Mia knew immediately what he was apologizing for and a chill ran up her spine as she tried to regain her strength. She raised her leg to knee him in the groin, but knowing that it was her only recourse, he anticipated her move and angled his body to the left, her knee barely scraping the side of his waist.

"We could have been happy Val, but at least we both know how the story will end now." He threw Mia against a wall that served as a small closet and went for the knife that lay on the floor less than a foot away. As he stooped down to reach for the knife, Mia bent and quickly kicked as hard as she could, striking Parker in the ribs. He was forced back toward the door, but held fast to the handrail beside the door. Mia ran a few steps, aiming for his windpipe, she kicked him again with another front snap kick. This time, Parker flew backwards out the small door and landed flat on his back, dazed. He scrambled to get back into the motorhome as Mia hurriedly closed and locked the door and got behind the steering wheel. Fortunately, the keys were still in the ignition. She turned the key, gunned the accelerator and was rewarded by the start of the engine.

"Thank you," she whispered. Quickly placing the gear in drive, the motorhome roared to life and jerked forward with the van in tow. Mia drove blindly leaving plumes of dust in her wake.

Parker lay dazed on the hard, wet earth being pummeled by the warm rain as the engine of the motorhome came to life. This was not how he had planned things. It seemed everything had gone terribly wrong. He couldn't let it end like this. With renewed strength, Parker sprung to his feet and ran after the van. He managed to catch hold of the rear van door and hop up on the fender. He had to get back into the motorhome before she reached the main highway.

Parker used the bumper of the van as a foothold and slipped twice on its slippery surface before finally obtaining the desired grip. He then splayed his arms out, clutching the van is if he were hugging it. With almost no effort, he hoisted himself on top of the moving van and carefully walked across its roof. When he reached the Winnebago, with catlike quickness and agility, he climbed the small, steel ladder on the back of the motorhome and attempted to open the hatch located on its roof. The hatch was a 16" x 16" inch square with a hooded top secured by two latches. But, the latches restricted how far the compartment could open.

Parker struggled with the hatch for a brief moment

and then kicked it loose. With a horrible screeching sound it toppled off the top of the motorhome, quickly disappearing in the cloud of dust left by the speeding vehicle. He then slipped into the Winnebago, landing on his haunches in the center of where it all began.

She could see the main highway roughly five miles ahead when she heard a thump on the roof of the motorhome. Afraid, she increased her speed to ninety-five miles per hour. There was no way that could be him. The sight of him sprawled on the ground was still in her mind.

Suddenly, she heard the sound of footsteps. She glanced in the rear-view mirror and froze. The sight of Parker making his way through the cabin area made her blood run cold. Two more miles. In two miles she would be on the main highway. People could see her and know she was alive—people whom she could ask for help. Mia's speed dropped drastically to fifty miles an hour when Parker placed a strangle hold on her neck. Her foot came free from the accelerator and her hands from the steering wheel as she kicked and flailed the air. Parker positioned himself behind her, choking off her air.

As Mia struggled to pry Parker's vice-like grip from around her neck, her foot once again met with the accelerator, pushing the speed past sixty miles an hour. There was a small ditch in the road where the red dirt and pavement met. The motorhome jumped the ditch, landing awkwardly on two wheels before traversing the solid, yellow line and continuing on all four wheels. The van disengaged and was left behind on the rocky earth.

Mia vacillated between the imminent deaths of dying at Parker's hands or from a horrible automobile accident as she punched and swung with her right hand and attempted to steer with her left. The Winnebago swerved blindly along the slick blacktop to the sounds of blaring horns and irate drivers. She felt the familiar despair of a losing battle as she fought for consciousness. It seemed no matter how badly the motorhome shook and shimmied, Parker's grip around her neck never faltered.

They came up fast on a turn in the highway and Mia knew that this was how her life would end. But, this time she accepted that fact. She stopped struggling and submitted as the motorhome crossed the opposite lane, flipped over the supporting guardrail, battering her body in the process. Images of her mother's face graced her thoughts and then flashes of her wedding day followed by a bright, welcoming light.

Parker's hands came free from Mia's throat when the Winnebago rammed into the guardrail, tumbled out of control and down the ravine.

"Mother," he screamed "you'd be proud of me."

The Winnebago rolled and tumbled as Parker and Mia were assaulted with the various items that had come free from the overhead cabinets and mini-refrigerator. All of Parker's medications, frozen dinners, glass, news clippings on Mia and other paraphernalia swirled around throughout the small cabin area before the motorhome came to rest on its side at the bottom of the ravine and burst into flames.

Chapter Eighteen

Edward busied himself in the kitchen. He mopped the floor, cleaned out the refrigerator and relined the shelves, something he promised Mia he would do almost a year ago. After his mother's visit, he made a decision: He had to get it together and start doing things for himself.

It would certainly be a hard transition to make, but he had been a bachelor for a long time before he met Mia. Since Mia's disappearance, he maintained a wonderful support system between the partner's wives at his job and in the beginning, Lynda. They had taken the liberty of making sure he was well fed. Eventually, he asked that the partners wives cease in having the meals prepared and delivered to his house. His mother had prepared several meals during her visit, but they were gone now and it was time to put his culinary skills to work.

He turned on the small, five inch, kitchen television and searched for a football game. When he found one, he retrieved a beer and a package of hamburger meat from the refrigerator and turned on one of the burners. He seasoned the lean ground beef and placed it in the cast-iron skill. Soon the aroma of sautéed onions, garlic and tomato sauce filled the air. Edward leaned back on the counter, not really paying attention to the football game playing in the background. He took a long sip of beer and let out an exasperated breath—melancholy setting in. As he stood, staring into space, the phone rang, intruding on his thoughts. Edward picked it up on the third ring.

"Hello," he answered solemnly.

"Well hello, stranger," the voice on the other end responded.

Edward had been dreading this moment since Lynda left his house almost a week ago. He rolled his eyes and cursed silently under his breath. He had received every message she left on his answering service but had never bothered to respond. He just didn't have it in him to get into some deep conversation about nothing, as far as he was concerned.

"Are you there?" Lynda asked.

"Yeah, I'm here. How are you Lynda?"

"I'm good," Lynda responded carefully, noting the tension in Edward's voice. "Look, I just wanted to call and touch base with you—no strings. 'Ya know I feel horrible about what happened, even though nothing *really* happened, but I'm sorry just the same. And, I just felt that at some point, I should call and clear the air. I don't want there to be any tension or awkwardness whenever we see each other."

"I appreciate that, Lynda. I really do," Edward said, thankful to be let off the hook.

"Great. So, how have you been holding up?"

"As best as can be expected under the circumstances, I guess."

"Well, that's good to hear."

"How about yourself?"

"Oh, I really can't complain. But, I really do miss my friend—our talks, workout sessions—just everything."

"I know, me too, Lynda."

"I'm sorry, I didn't mean to call and bring you down."

"No, no that's okay. Anyway, I don't think that's possible. But, I'm glad we had the opportunity to clear the air."

"Me too. So, are there any new developments in the case?"

"There's been a warrant issued. This Parker McKinley guy is obviously on the run."

"With Mia?," Lynda gasped.

"That's the assumption, although they're saying they just want to talk to him at this point."

"Talk to him? "Well, when they went to his house,

were they able to gather anything to help them with the case?"

"I'm pretty sure they didn't. I found the area where he lived at before the police did and I didn't find anything."

"What? How did you manage that?"

"Well, I won't go into the specifics of how I obtained the information, but I did. And, when I went there, it was just this partially abandoned trailer park of sorts."

"So has anyone seen them together?"

"No, that's the problem. No one has seen Mia since she was on the plane."

"Edward?"

"Yeah," Edward responded with obvious distraction.

"What does all of this mean?"

"It doesn't mean a damned thing, because the police don't have proof that he has Mia."

"Do the police still think Mia is alive—particularly since this guy has uprooted his home and is on the run now?"

Edward paused for a long while and then spoke haltingly. "Lynda, they honestly don't know."

"Then what do you believe?"

"I believe that I *have* to believe she's still alive—it's the only thing that keeps me going—that sliver of hope that she may still be alive."

"I'm so sorry, Edward."

"I know. Hey look, I have some work I need to finish up here," he said, attempting to sound more upbeat. "I'll let you know if I hear anything."

"Please do. And Edward?"

"Yeah?"

"You take care of yourself."

"I will."

Edward disconnected the line and turned the fire off under his spaghetti sauce. He took another long swallow of beer, finishing it off, and squeezed the bridge of his nose. He thought about his conversation with Lynda and wondered if he really believed that his wife was alive or whether he just gave the answer that was expected of him. He turned off the television and the house was enveloped in silence. Suddenly, he wasn't in the mood to cook, eat or watch the game. He sluggishly climbed the stairs and entered the master bedroom, where he fell across the bed. Sleep whispered seductively in his ear, promising a temporary reprieve from his pain and despair. He willingly acquiesced to its allure.

Lynda reclined on her couch and pondered the conversation she'd had with Edward. She felt terrible for what her friend Mia must be going through The fear. The horror and most of all, the uncertainty of whether she would live or die, if the latter hadn't already happened. But, because Edward was here and she could see and hear his pain, she felt worse for him. A part of her wanted to run to him, hold him in her arms and love his worries away—just make him forget for a little while. The other part of her knew that would never happen and she must never breath a word of her feelings or act upon them ever again. No one would ever know her true feelings for Edward Simone.

Michael was a wonderful guy, but it seemed that she needed to remind herself of that whenever she thought of Edward. On the other hand, she knew that if she ever wanted to have a meaningful relationship, she was going to have to get past her obsession with Edward.

She and Michael had finally taken their relationship to the next level and it had been everything she expected and more. Her three day, two night stay at the beautiful Beverly Hills Hotel had catered to her every whim and imaginable dream. Michael had reserved an amazing grand, deluxe bungalow suite set in lush hibiscus, blooming bougainvillea and tropical palms. Lynda felt like she was on an exotic, tropical island. The wood-burning fireplace, private patio and Jacuzzi tub was an added bonus that she just couldn't pull herself away from. Although they had a personal butler, one night while she relaxed in the Jacuzzi, Michael took advantage of the gourmet kitchen and dining room within the bungalow by showing off his culinary skills. Lynda had been surprised that she'd shown no hesitation in revealing her hearty appetite in front of Michael. The lobster tails, succulent crab cakes and Caesar salad had left her craving the recipe and Michael. Initially, he was not willing to part with it, but after their intense lovemaking session, he would have told her government secrets, had he known any.

Lynda smiled thinking back to the two blissful nights that had taken place. What she hadn't expected was that he would still be around and she would still be floating from that magical weekend. She found herself missing him when they weren't in each other's presence or talking on the phone. He was currently on a business trip overseeing the plans of his project in New York and she had to admit to herself that she missed him more than she thought she would. She was falling fast and knew there was no turning back now.

Although she knew Michael could never be Edward, her mind was made up that she would take a chance and see where this relationship took her. She had been hurt many times in the past, but she would always wonder 'What if?' if she did not pursue this relationship. The fact was, that people often wanted things they couldn't have or that wasn't good for them and she was no different.

With the many attributes Michael possessed, she still couldn't rid herself of this apprehension. He was tall, handsome, single, an excellent cook with a terrific job, who seemed to really care about her. Was she losing her mind? The fact that she had to debate whether or not to get involved with someone as great as Michael said a lot about her state of mind.

Lynda opened the sliding glass door and walked out onto the balcony adjacent to her bedroom, which overlooked Santa Monica Boulevard. She observed the passersby hustling to and fro in the warm summer weather, snuggling up next to each other and took particular interest in the number of couples she counted. *What kind of bitter old woman was I becoming*, she thought grimly. She had become so desensitized to love and relationships, other than Mia's, that it now appeared she was seeing the world for the first time— through the eyes of a first-time lover. She looked on at the young and seasoned lovers, not with envy, but rather with a renewed outlook on love and an assurance that she too, could have the same thing—if only she would reach out and accept it.

She heard a phone ringing in the distance and realized that it was hers. Rushing, she came in and slid the door closed behind her. Hoping to make it to the phone before the answering machine picked up, Lynda answered on the third ring with a breathless,

"Hello."

"Hey baby."

"Michael. Hi."

"Did I catch you at a bad time?"

"Don't be silly. I was just out on the balcony when I heard the phone ringing and I had to run to get it."

"Well, I just want to make sure that I'm the only one making you breathless."

"Oooh, stop it now. You're not playing fair. If you were here maybe you'd be singing a different tune."

"You're right. I'd be putting my money where my mouth is."

"And I hope that would be all over me."

"Keep talking like that and I'll be on the first thing flying out of here."

"I hope so."

They both laughed and then enjoyed the comfortable silence.

"Do you know how much I miss you?"

"Probably not half as much as I miss you. Oh boy, I can't believe I said that."

"Believe it because I feel the same way."

"Oh Michael. So when are you coming home?"

"Music to my ears. I'll be coming in on a 6:45 p.m. flight on Friday."

"Would you like me to pick you up from the airport?"

"I'd like that a lot. I'll call you Friday morning with the flight number and maybe we can grab some take out and go back to my place."

"Now, that sounds like a plan. I can't wait."

"Okay, baby. I'll talk to you on Friday. Good night."

"Good night."

Lynda, curled up under the down comforter on her queen-sized bed, all thoughts of Edward pushed back to the far recesses of her mind. She imagined that her silk gown were Michael's hands, gently caressing her body and she could almost feel his lips and tongue slowly sucking the side of her slender neck. She breathed deeply. Yes, she was ready to accept the love that was due her.

Chapter Nineteen

The bright, warm glow gently carried her away. Her body, a weightless mass of tissue and cells. Without any particular destination—except towards the light, she continued floating at a steady, calming pace. Although there was no concept of time, in what seemed much too soon, she reached the omnipresent glow. Unafraid and with an overwhelming sense of belonging, she reached out to touch the glow. The tips of her fingers just barely began to caress the assuaging presence. It felt right—where she belonged and she was accepting of the gift that was to be hers....

Her body jerked convulsively in response to the defibrillator's charge.

"There she is! We got her back!" yelled the paramedic monitoring the screen. "She's really lucky to have been thrown from the vehicle," he said as he and a female paramedic hurriedly placed the lady on a gurney and hoisted her into the back of the ambulance.

"Yep, sure is. That person there should've been so lucky," the female paramedic said angling her head in the direction of the badly burned body that had been pulled from the still smoldering wreckage. The paramedic climbed in behind the wheel and the female paramedic climbed in the back with the still unconscious lady.

"You're going to be just fine," she whispered as she pulled the thin blanket up to her shoulders. Siren blaring, the ambulance sped away from the scene leaving behind several police vehicles, two fire engines and the charred remains of Parker McKinley.

Mia woke to a bright glow. Only this time, it wasn't a calming light, but rather an irritating, painful light that loomed over her. As she blinked repeatedly to clear her vision, she realized it was a pen light and that her eyes were being held open. She turned her head because to move either of her arms seemed to require too much effort.

"Welcome back." Mia heard. She turned her head and with clearer vision, focused in on a friendly-looking man in a white jacket with dark brown hair that was graying at the temples and a neatly trimmed mustache. She surmised him to be a doctor.

"I knew you were a fighter," he said.

"What?" Mia croaked and the attending nurse quickly brought a straw to her lips. The water was the best thing she could ever remember tasting. She took several sips and swallowed hard. The doctor waited patiently for her and then continued

"I'm Dr. Ferguson and I said, I knew you were a fighter. Pretty bad accident you were in."

"Yeah," was all she could manage as she tried to scoot up on the pillow. "Ooow."

A nurse propped her pillows and helped her into a more comfortable position.

"Where am I?"

"You're in Nevada General. Take it easy now. You've been in a coma for most of the day, due to a very bad blow to your skull when you were ejected from the vehicle. I actually expected you to be out a lot longer. Also, your left arm is broken and one of your ribs on the same side. Lots of bruises and swelling, but otherwise no permanent damage."

"I thought I'd died."

"Officially you had. You were gone for a full ninety-seven seconds."

"It was amazingly peaceful. Nothing like I would have expected."

"That's interesting. Most people say that, but when asked what they expected death to be like, they never know. Anyway, if it hadn't been for one of your biggest fans here," Dr. Ferguson said pointing to the nurse that had not spoken a word that Mia could remember. "We would have tagged you as a Jane Doe."

"I don't understand," Mia asked confused.

"Well, you didn't have any identification on you. Most people who are homeless or without I.D. and require medical attention are labeled as John or Jane Doe. But, Nurse Bennett here recognized you right away—Mia Simone. Even with all the bruises."

Mia managed a half-smile. *Fans*, she thought. It was an alleged fan that had her in this horrible predicament. She supposed she couldn't judge the entire world by the actions of one, but she did know that she would probably be suspicious of people for the rest of her life.

"Thank you." She nodded in the direction of Nurse Bennett, a tall, thin woman with a bland countenance with the exception of the bright, pink lipstick she wore. Nurse Bennett offered a wide, warm smile, for the first time Mia noted.

"Has my husband been notified?"

"By now he should have. Since you don't have a listed number, we contacted the LA County Sheriff's Department who promised they would let him know immediately. Apparently, you've been through quite an ordeal. We were shocked to learn that you had been kidnapped and—" he said glancing at her forearm and noting the old cigarette burns and rope abrasions on her wrists. "Apparently, tortured as well."

Mia turned her head toward the window and fought back the onslaught of tears she felt building. As if sensing her thoughts, Dr. Ferguson spoke gently and soothingly.

"You're okay now, Mia. He's dead. Whoever he was—Whoever did this to you is dead. Burned up in the motorhome. It'll be another day or so before the coroner's report is released."

Mia cried silently as the tears flowed in a steady stream, unchecked down her cheeks. Her crying built to a crescendo as deep sobs began to rack her body. Sensing that she needed this time alone, Dr. Ferguson stood and motioned to Nurse Bennett to leave.

"You try and get some rest now. Call the nurse if you need anything," he said as he gently squeezed her hand and placed her chart back at the foot of the bed.

Mia cried like a baby. She cried freely for all that she had endured. She cried thoroughly to purge herself of the horrific experience she had survived. But most importantly, she cried and gave thanks to her Maker for being by her side and for bringing her through the darkness and despair of her situation. It was hard for her to believe that this ordeal was finally over, she was still alive and shortly would be reunited with her husband. She thought of his handsome face and couldn't wait to be safely in his arms again. Soon, she drifted off into a fretful, disruptive sleep.

Parker's badly burned, lifeless body remained alive in her dreams as he chased her relentlessly, finding her no matter where she hid. A deafening sound in her head, *klunk, klunk, klunk*. Her legs were heavy and she looked down to discover they were weighted down with a typewriter attached to her ankles, supported by shackles. The entire time, Parker behind her asking, "What is the ending, Mia?" She kept her head straight as she hobbled along trying to get away, but stole a glance when she no longer heard him or the familiar *klunk, klunk, klunk*. She breathed deeply, hoping that he had disappeared, but to her surprise, he was right behind her, holding the typewriter, his face burned to a blackened crisp.

"Nooooo!" Mia screamed as she came fully awake, sweat beading her brow. She relaxed slightly on her pillows, her heart still beating rapidly. "It was just a dream," she whispered to herself. "Just a dream."

Edward sat at his office computer crunching numbers for an upcoming acquisition their company was about to embark upon. Lately, he had practically been living at the office. Under normal circumstances he might have complained to his wife about putting in fourteen to fifteen hours a day, but these were far from normal circumstances and as a result, he was thankful for the grueling hours. Each day when he reached home, it was after 9:00 p.m. Bone weary, he would have just barely enough strength to make himself a sandwich, stand over the kitchen sink while eating it and fall across his bed fully clothed only to wake up the next morning at 5:00 a.m. and do it all over again.

He squinted at the screen, concentrating on the numbers before him. His assistant tapped lightly on the door before walking in.

"Edward, got a minute?"

Edward looked up from the computer screen and wiped his tired eyes. "Yeah sure Nathalie, come on in."

Nathalie came in with her steno pad and signature folder under her arm and took a seat at the small conference table in Edward's office. "I need to have you approve these invoices," she said, handing him the red signature folder. Edward opened the folder and began signing the invoices.

"You know, I don't think I ever properly thanked you for that favor you did for me. I really appreciate it."

"Don't even think about it, it was my pleasure."

"Well, let's see what we have here, whew! $288,000 for the pilots salary for six months. I'm in the wrong business."

"I used to think that too, but those guys earn their money, especially here. When Mr. Kincaid or Mr. Blake want to leave for Europe or wherever, they don't care what the pilots are doing, what time of day it is—they just want to go, now. Also, I've done some research and found that the average pilot makes $200-$250,000.00 per year starting out and that's with a some-what normal schedule. So, $288,000.00 is probably fair."

"Yeah, I guess when you put it that way."

"Anyway, if you were a pilot, who else would I work for?"

"Come on now. You're one of the sharpest assistants here. I'm sure you'd have no problem getting another job. An even better question is if you weren't here, who would put up with me?"

"You've got a point there, boss."

They both laughed and Nathalie took note that it was the first time in a long time for Edward.

"You know, it's good to see you smile again."

Edward turned serious, "Yeah, I guess at some point you have to," he said thoughtfully.

"Well, I have one more thing," Nathalie said, sensing the shift in the atmosphere. "Mr. Kincaid and Blake would like to meet with you and the Board members today from 11:00 to 1:00 p.m. in the conference room. Lunch will be served."

"Okay. An emergency Board meeting, just what I need."

Nathalie stood to leave and Edward handed her the folder.

"Anything I need to prepare for the meeting?"

"Yes, as a matter of fact there is. I'm going to e-mail this document to you and then I'd like you to make them into overheads and make ten hard copies for handouts."

"Sure thing. I'll be waiting for it."

Edward turned in his swivel chair and continued punching numbers into his calculator, applying the finishing touches to his presentation. Originally, the document was to be for Robert Kincaid's eyes only. Now, he was going to have to make a full-fledged presentation, he just knew it. Although Bob would never say it, this was his way of making sure Edward was on top of his due diligence for the acquisition—and he certainly planned to be. He punched in an equation that gave him satisfactory figures and then typed them into the graph he was working on. He saved the document, opened Outlook, made it an attachment and sent it to Nathalie marked 'Urgent.'

"Yes," he mumbled to himself enthusiastically.

He stood, stretched and then retrieved a pair of handgrips from his drawer. As he systematically squeezed and flexed his hand, he stared out the window at the expansive view. The last time he had actually taken time to enjoy the view was when he had spoken to Mia from the airport. Turning away from the window, his eyes came to rest on the picture of Mia that sat on his desk. He thought about what his mother said to him during her visit. He certainly hoped she was right because his faith was beginning to waiver. Reluctantly returning to his desk, he decided to go through some of the mail that had piled up during the week. Before he sifted through half the pile, his intercom buzzed.

"Yes, Nathalie?"

"Sergeant Williams is on line one."

"Okay, thanks."

Edward tried to slow his heart rate down a bit before he picked up the line. Every time the sergeant called, he felt like his heart was about to explode in his chest. The anticipation of the news he might hear was almost more than he could bear. He slowly picked up the receiver, cleared his throat and depressed the flashing, green button.

"Sergeant Williams."

"Edward, I got a call from the Nevada County Sheriff's Department about fifteen minutes ago—"

"Edward could hear his heart beating in his ears like a drum. He clutched the receiver until he felt cramping in his hand. He couldn't speak or form a clear thought, but he knew that it seemed as though Sergeant Williams was deliberately talking slower. Or, it could have been that he was speaking but Edward just didn't hear him. Edward seemed to come back to the present and he heard the shuffling of papers.

"Your wife is in Nevada County General."

"Is she—"

"And yes, she's alive."

"Oh, thank God. Thank God. I can't believe it. How is she?"

"I believe she's just fine, but she was in a bad car accident. Just get your butt up there and see," the sergeant said encouragingly.

"Yeah right. Right. Hey, thanks a lot—for everything."

"Don't mention it. I'm just relieved this has a happy ending. You take it easy."

"Thanks. You do the same."

Edward hung up the phone almost uncertain of what to do next. He stood up and then sat back at his desk for a moment. He grabbed his suit jacket and headed out the door towards Nathalie's desk.

"Nathalie page the pilots and tell them to get the corporate jet ready to go to Nevada."

A puzzled expression came over Nathalie's face, but she kept her calm demeanor.

"When should I tell them to be ready?"

"In thirty minutes. I'm on my way to the airport right now."

"What if I can't—"

"Make it happen, now Nathalie," Edward said abruptly.

"Okay," Nathalie responded, taken a little off guard "And what about the presentation at 11:00?" Nathalie inquired as Edward reached the elevator.

"Call Harvey. Hell, I don't care, think of something," Edward yelled as the elevator doors closed.

Nathalie didn't dare ask her boss where he was going, but she had an idea that it had something to do with his wife. Something told her she wouldn't be seeing him for a while.

Chapter Twenty

The dimly lit halls took Edward back to a time of old television movies he'd seen many years ago. The walls were always some awful color of green, yellow or something that used to be white, and the halls were always empty during the night. He found a nurse on duty at the nurse's station that gave him Mia's room number, but not before she asked for his identification to make sure he was a relative. Another nurse named Bennett advised him that it was okay and that the doctor would be back on duty in another hour or so to talk to him and answer any questions he might have.

Edward continued down the hall looking left to right, in search of room 117. Moments later, he was standing directly in front of the door with a hesitancy he couldn't understand. He had been waiting for what seemed like forever to find his wife and now his feet felt like cement blocks. For the first time since he was a small boy, he was scared—really and truly scared. Even when he knew Mia had been the victim of foul play, he hadn't been this scared. Then, there was something that enabled him to create his own outcome and it was that Mia was going to be okay. But now, no matter what image he created, on the other side of this door would be the truth—that he had failed her.

He willed his feet to move, slowly placing one in front of the other. The door was slightly ajar. He slowly pushed it open and quietly entered the semi-private room. Mia was the only person there. Edward stopped mid-way between the door and Mia's bed, shocked by what he saw. Mia appeared dwarfed as she lay sleeping peacefully in the hospital bed. She had two black eyes, one of which appeared swollen shut. On her forehead was a large, purplish-blue knot, almost the size of a golf ball and her lower lip had been split. Her face appeared drawn and her hair was matted and flat. Edward stood there, afraid to touch her.

As if sensing a presence, Mia opened one of her eyes. For a moment she thought she might be dreaming. But then, she felt the familiar touch of Edward's warm, strong hand and knew it was real. She tried to sit up, but was stricken with a searing pain in her chest and forced back into her previous position.

"Edward," she whispered.

"It's okay, baby. I'm here and I'm not leaving your side," Edward said reassuringly as he leaned over her. His eyes brimmed with tears as he thought of the agony his wife must be in. He was much too hurt to be angry right now about the circumstances that placed his wife in this horrible situation.

Mia began to cry, "Oh Edward, I thought I'd never see you again. I was so scared."

"I know Mia. But, baby it's all over now. I'm so sorry I didn't come with you. If I had, this never would have happened," Edward said as he kissed Mia gently on the forehead. "I'm just so thankful God brought you back to me," he managed through tears.

They held each other for a long time. The only sounds to be heard were those of their sniffles and muffled cries.

There was a quick knock on the door and Dr. Ferguson appeared. Edward grabbed a few tissues from the tray table nearby and quickly tried to compose himself.

"Oh, I'm sorry. I didn't mean to intrude," Dr. Ferguson said apologetically.

"That's all right," Edward said clearing his throat. "You must be the doctor."

"Yes, I am. Dr. Ferguson. And, you must be Edward," he said, extending his hand.

Edward shook his hand and stood over to the side as Dr. Ferguson reviewed Mia's chart. The doctor felt Mia's glands and studied the dilation of her pupils with his pen-light. He then turned so that he would be facing both Edward and Mia.

"Well, I'm sure you have questions, Mr. Simone, but let me start by saying that it's not as bad as it looks. The black eyes are from a blow she received to the skull when she was ejected from the vehicle. As you can see by the gauze on her forehead there are cuts and abrasions. She has a broken rib on the left side and a broken arm. She was in a coma for almost twenty-four hours and that's the only reason why we haven't released her yet."

"Well, when do you think she'll be able to go home?"

"That was going to be my question," Mia interjected.

Dr. Ferguson grinned broadly, "Well, there doesn't seem to be anything else we can do for her here. But, just the same, I'd like to keep you here until morning. Additionally, there's some paper work I need to have you or your husband fill out, like your regular doctor's name and address. I'll forward all your test results and paper work to him and he should be able to remove your cast in six to eight weeks."

"So there'll be no permanent damage from the coma she was in?" Edward asked.

"No, not that we can see. Her MRI was clean. Like I told her when she first came in, she's one lucky lady."

The jet seemed to glide across the predominantly, clear skies. Nevada became a patchwork of brown, green and rust colored swatches that reminded Edward of an old quilt. He had never been happier to leave a place in his entire life. Although it was only a short distance and a forty-five minute flight, it seemed like forever before they would reach the sanctity of their home, together.

Mia wanted to snuggle into Edward's side but the cast made it difficult for them. She felt like she could live forever in the comfort and security of his arms. A chill ran up her spine at the thought of her ordeal with Parker McKinley.

"You okay, babe?"

"I'm fine, just a little chilled is all."

Edward knew Mia was being haunted by her experience. He had spoken privately with Dr. Ferguson about the side effects of this type of ordeal. Dr. Ferguson informed him that it was not uncommon for some people to have bad, recurring dreams related to their experience. Others might experience anxiety attacks when outside of their home, even in broad daylight. And then, he continued, some had no outward symptoms at all. But, Edward didn't think the latter would apply to Mia. He was going to have to find some way to make her feel secure again—to become the independent spirit she used to be. In many ways, she was the same Mia, yet in other ways, that only a spouse could recognize, there was a part of her that had been stripped bare and made vulnerable.

This morning, Edward had planned to go to the nearest mall and buy her some clothing to wear home, but Mia panicked when he tried to leave her side. When Edward looked into her beautiful, gray eyes, he knew he could not leave her. In them, were fear, desperation and fire—the same fire that had brought her back to him. The same fire that revealed she was a fighter, but right now required his nurturing and reassurance.

Nurse Bennett, who had witnessed the entire scene, happily offered to shop for Mia as soon as the stores opened. However, Edward was not ready to relinquish any power to another potential 'fan,' even if she was the nurse. He kindly refused and called Nathalie to arrange to have a personal shopper pick out comfortable, casual attire and deliver it to the hospital.

"Edward, would this be a size six?" Nathalie asked excitedly.

"Hmmm. This time I think it should be about a size four," he replied. Edward quickly filled Nathalie in on the details of finding Mia and asked that she let the office know.

Nathalie was more than happy to comply.

"Fortunately, the shopping service we used here for Valentine's Day has offices in 42 states. I'll make sure the clothing is there within the next couple of hours."

"Thanks a lot, Nathalie. I'll touch base with you soon."

"Oh Edward?"

"Yeah?"

"I'm glad Mia is back safely."

"Thanks, Nathalie—me too."

Before noon, Nurse Bennett brought in a neatly wrapped, brown package which had been delivered. Edward was surprised that the personal shopper had proved to have pretty good taste in clothing, or it very well could have been Nathalie. In any event, the instructions had been followed to the letter with color, size and taste. With sunglasses, a pair of khakis, a black and brown lambswool sweater, Rockport walking shoes, bra, panties, and a pair of socks. Everything fit Mia perfectly; however, she looked like a battered child with her hair pulled back in a ponytail, no make-up and considerable amount of weight loss.

As they sailed across the sky, Mia rested her head on his chest, sleeping soundly. Edward was sure it was the first real sleep she'd had in weeks. As he gently smoothed her light, brown hair, he noticed several strands of gray that had not been there before. His heart ached for his wife. They had not discussed any particulars surrounding her ordeal. He understood that she was not ready to talk about it so soon and he didn't plan to push. But, at some point, he hoped that she would be willing to open up to him and share this very personal experience.

Edward thought back to his conversation with Dr. Ferguson. He confirmed that she had not been sexually assaulted and that Parker McKinley was beyond the shadow of a doubt, dead. That alone, made Edward feel that they would both be able to get through this ordeal a little easier.

The pilot announced their descent into Los Angeles, pulling Edward from his thoughts. Mia never moved, but rather continued to lie motionless in a deep sleep on his chest. Edward kissed her softly on the tip of her nose.

"It's going to be okay, now," he whispered softly in her ear. "You're safe."

Edward unlocked the door and escorted Mia into their house. She stood in the foyer for a long moment before deciding to take the two steps into the sunken living room.

"I can't believe it," she said with childlike wonder.

"Can't believe what?"

"That the house is still clean," she joked for the first time.

They laughed together and it was music to Edward's ears. He gazed at her and drew her to him, pulling her chin up to face him. Slowly, he removed the sunglasses from her face and she turned away, embarrassed.

"Don't," Edward whispered reassuringly. "You're at home and it's okay. I don't care about the bumps and bruises, you will always be beautiful to me, no matter what—because I love you."

Tears began to flow in a steady stream down Mia's face. Edward gently wiped them away with the pads of his thumbs.

"Whenever you're ready to talk, I'm here baby. I'm right here. And, I'm not leaving your side until I know you're okay."

Mia could only nod her head as Edward held her in his arms.

"Why don't we get you upstairs and into a hot bath."

"That sounds good." Mia replied.

Edward helped her up the spiral staircase and into the master bedroom suite. She sat down on the chaise while he ran her bath. Before long, Mia lay immersed in the hot, sudsy water with her left arm propped up on the side of the tub, hoping to soak the events of her experience away. She was happy to be home, yet she felt like a stranger who had been gone far too long. The feeling of uneasiness seemed unshakable. She knew Parker was dead, but there was a part of him that would live forever in her memory. *How will I ever get past this*? she silently asked herself as she stared blankly at the tiled wall before her.

Edward stood at the kitchen stove warming chicken noodle soup. He poured it into a bowl and added it to a plate that contained a turkey sandwich for Mia. The phone rang and he let the answering machine pick it up. He didn't want any disturbances. But, he heard his mother's voice and grabbed the phone up in mid-sentence. Apparently, she had phoned his office and been told by Nathalie that he had gone to get Mia.

"Hello, mother," Edward spoke excitedly into the phone.

"You're back. I spoke with Nathalie and I just praised God when she told me. I knew it."

"Yeah, your faith never wavered."

"How is she?"

"A little bruised and battered, but I think she'll be okay."

"That's wonderful. Wait a minute, your dad wants to speak with you."

"Hi son? I heard the good news. It's a blessing."

"It certainly is," Edward answered carefully. His

father had always been able to gauge him —actually see right through him.

"So, Mia is doin' okay?"

"Yeah, she's a little bruised, like I told mom, but she's going to be fine."

"Son?"

"Yeah dad?"

"I sense something else is going on. You wanna tell me about it?"

"Maybe another time, dad. Maybe another time."

Chapter Twenty-One

Edward had been feeling both happy and uneasy over the past two months since Mia had been back home, but just assumed that it was stress and delight—that is until he spoke with his father. He and his mother had always been closer than he and his father. But, his father had always possessed the uncanny ability to get behind his shield and to the heart of whatever was going on with him.

Edward Simone, Sr. was like a bloodhound when he sensed that something was wrong. And, he was especially keen when it came to pinpointing problems with his son. He pulled no punches—just as he had done during their last conversation more than a month ago. There had been no point in trying to deny anything. His father knew something was wrong and did not plan on hanging up the phone until he got it out of him.

Edward described what had happened between he and Lynda, of course leaving out the more graphic details. His father listened quietly on the other end and then in his usual one sentence responses, he said, "Well son, men will be tempted. The point is you didn't go all the way with it, so let your conscience be your guide."

"Thanks dad." Had been Edward's response, but inside he was thinking What! Did you even hear what I said?"

As he sat in the waiting room of the doctor's office with Mia, he had to admit that he felt better after talking to his father. Just admitting it to someone that he could trust lifted a tremendous weight from his shoulders. But more importantly, he identified that the uneasy feeling he'd been having was guilt. Pure and simple.

"A penny for your thoughts," Mia said as she squeezed his hand.

"My thoughts are worth a lot more than that, " he

joked.

"Well is that so?"

"Yeah, it is," Edward said as he kissed her on the forehead. "No, actually I was just thinking of how glad I am to have you back and to have this time with you."

"Even if it's sitting in a doctor's office?" Mia asked.

"Absolutely," Edward grinned.

Mia smiled and it seemed to light up the room. Edward could see that Mia was on her way to a full recovery. She had begun to joke more and make the quick, sassy comebacks that he loved and was so accustomed to. The cuts and bruises had healed. He had washed her hair many times with her favorite shampoo and conditioner and now it was shiny, lustrous and bouncy—the way it used to be. Today her cast was being removed and Edward felt this would chip away the final layer of the obvious physical abuse. Now, the emotional healing could really begin.

"Mia Simone," the nurse called.

Mia and Edward followed a middle-aged, petite nurse to an exam room. Edward took a chair in the corner while the nurse helped Mia up on the table.

"I'm just going to take your blood pressure and temperature and the doctor will be right in to remove your cast."

"Thanks," Mia replied.

As Mia and Edward waited for the doctor, Mia said, "Wow! You know it just dawned on me that my cast isn't even signed."

"Well, it's just been the two of us since you've been home, babe."

"I don't know. I mean I've only spoken to Lynda twice. I thought she'd come by, but she mentioned that she wanted to give us our time alone before she started bombarding me with visits. Even your folks haven't come by."

"Well, that's perfectly normal, don't you think?"

Edward asked, his pulse elevating just a notch as his mind flashed back to a virtually nude Lynda in his living room.

"Anyway, my parents will be here in another week or so and you'll regret you ever wanted them here," Edward joked.

"Stop it," Mia said laughing despite her best efforts. "I know, just feeling melancholy I guess. When I was fourteen, I broke my arm sliding into third base."

"Wait a minute, back up. You mean you played baseball?"

"Well, softball. That's what girls play in school."

"I never knew you were a tomboy."

"Sure was."

Edward pulled out his pen, walked over to Mia and began to write on her cast. When he was done, 'I Love You, Ed' had been scrawled across her cast.

"Even though it will be off in a minute, I hope it makes you feel better."

"It does," Mia said, a smile reaching her eyes.

The doctor entered with a small, saw-like device and within minutes the cast cracked in two. He then pulled each piece away from Mia's arm and brushed away the remaining remnants of plaster. He cleaned it with antiseptic wipes and then massaged the arm with lotion.

"There you go. Just take it easy for a few days, don't pick up anything too heavy or over exert the arm. However, do make sure to exercise it and you should be as good as new."

"Thank you, doctor," Mia said as the doctor closed the door behind him.

Edward had changed his position from the chair in the corner when the doctor began to massage her arm. He now stood over her with a horrified look on his face, as his gaze became fixated on the cigarette burns on her forearm.

"Mia, I think it's time for us to talk."

###

"—And that was the last thing I remember."

"I can't believe it," Edward said through clenched teeth and watery eyes. "I had no idea that you had been through such a horrible, horrible experience."

"Yeah," Mia said as she dabbed at her eyes with a tissue.

"Oh, baby. Come here," Edward said, pulling Mia into his arms. They stared at the fire in companionable silence.

"You know, I'm sure the fact that he's dead doesn't make it any easier for you, because it doesn't for me. I'm still very angry and I feel like I need to see someone brought to justice—made to suffer."

"I know. But, justice has been served. He's dead. My biggest issue is that I kept hearing people say how lucky I was, but the truth is I wasn't."

"What do you mean?"

"I mean, it simply wasn't my time to go."

"You're talking about when you saw the bright glow you mentioned right after the motorhome went over the cliff?"

"Yes and no. I know I was clinically dead for a minute or two, but then again, I wasn't. I knew that I wasn't—gone. I was somewhere in between. My fate was being decided."

"Hmmmm."

"And, the other thing is that he had so many opportunities to kill me. He had a knife, a gun that I never knew about until almost the end, he could have strangled me or even poisoned me. He could have just done anything that he wanted to do—but he didn't succeed in doing so."

"But it was also you. You never made it easy for him. Sometimes the thrill is in the fight and if there's no fight, then what's the point."

Mia sniffled and laughed awkwardly.

"What's so funny?"

"I was just thinking of how much you sound like your father."

"I hope that's a good thing."

"It's a very good thing. You sound so confident and reassuring."

"Because you know it's right."

"Yeah, I tried to keep strong and positive, but it was like screaming in the woods. Eventually, you wonder will anyone hear your screams?"

"Yes, but somebody just might. They might hear you or even see you. You never know."

"I guess you're right. I'm just ready to try and move on—get my life back on track."

"Oh, that reminds me. The check came today from the insurance company for your car. Of course it doesn't cover the full amount, but it will certainly help towards the new one."

"Uh huh," Mia replied thoughtfully.

"So, are you up to some shopping or what?"

"I think that's a wonderful way to get back on track." Mia smiled and Edward's heart swelled.

"Great. Why don't we grab some lunch at Spago's and then head over to the Lexus dealership."

"You just lead the way."

The forecasted rain never came to pass. In fact, the sky was partly cloudy with patches of dark blue here and there. Mia and Edward sat in her brand-new, hunter green Lexus SC400 Coupe on the edge of a dirt road over-looking Hollywood Lake. It was a place they visited frequently during their dating years. However, after getting married and nurturing their careers, they had become too busy to make the long drive from Sherman Oaks.

Mia and Edward relaxed in their reclined seats and watched as the sun seemingly disappeared into the water.

"We have to start doing this more often. It's very soothing," Mia said stroking Edward's cheek.

"I agree. I'd almost forgotten how beautiful this place was."

"I think my experience has taught me to stop and smell the roses. We had and still have a pretty good life, but I think for me, the humility was missing. It's certainly there now and I plan on taking nothing for granted."

It was Edward's turn to stroke Mia's cheek. "Mia you've been through so much. I think from this whole thing I've learned to have a deeper appreciation for you. You are *my* hero, Mia and I love you. I just wish I could erase that part of your life."

"I love you too and I can't thank you enough for never giving up. For taking care of me and nursing me back to a healthy mental state. I simply couldn't ask for a more loving husband."

They held hands, silent for a moment, just enjoying the quietude.

"I think I'm going to write about my experience."

Edward hesitated for a moment. "Do you think you want to relive all of that?"

"I think I have to. In the long run, I think only continued healing can come of it."

"I guess you're right. But, just be sure it's what you want. You know I support you one hundred percent."

"I know and that's why I can relive this again, because you'll be there. This book will be different from the fictional types I've written in the past. It'll be more of a self-help book that helps women through crisis."

"I think that's a really good direction to go. When will you start writing again? I know you still have the manuscript you sent to your agent before this happened."

"I know, she's called a couple of times and I just really wanted to make sure I was healed enough to deal with people. I just wasn't ready, but I intend to start returning some calls this week. Re-establishing those old ties and making some new ones."

Edward's stomach did a small somersault. He knew that included Lynda, but he truly believed that Lynda would not want to hurt Mia in that way. He nodded his head in agreement.

"Next we'll need to get you another laptop. I'm sure you'll be traveling again."

"Yeah," Mia shook her head uncertainly.

"But, I'll be right there with you, every step of the way. Or, until you get tired of me."

"That'll never happen," Mia said as she reached over and kissed Edward softly on the lips. "But, let's be realistic, you won't always be able to travel with me."

Edward let out an exasperated breath. "Well, whenever I'm not able to travel with you, you'll just have to have a media escort. Deal?"

"Deal."

"So, you ready to take us home?"

"Wait a minute," Mia joked. "Do you smell that?"

Edward sniffed the air and turned to Mia with a puzzled expression.

"I don't smell anything. What?"

"Take another whiff. It's brand new leather," Mia said as the engine purred. She laughed happily out loud as she put the car in drive. It was the seductive, throaty laugh that Edward remembered. The same one that had enchanted and seduced him—it was music to his ears. He chimed in with his deep baritone as they sped down the highway.

Chapter Twenty-Two

"Okay Anita that is just wonderful news, thanks again for everything. I'll E-mail you the synopsis in about a week or so. Oh and thank you for the lovely flowers. Okay, bye now."

Mia pressed the off button on the phone and leaned back in her chair. Over the past few days, she had returned many calls only to receive voice mails and answering machines. It was her turn now to receive calls and her phone had been ringing of the hook all morning. She had spoken with her mother-in-law, Dr. Fischer, Lynda and her agent, Anita. However, her conversation with Lynda had been the most interesting. She and Lynda had spoken a couple of times over the past couple of weeks and become reacquainted. Mia didn't realize how much she missed her friend until she found herself laughing so hard that her sides hurt. Like old times, they laughed, cried, gossiped and attended Billy Blank's Tae Bo class.

Mia had been surprised to learn that her good friend had become so seriously involved with this Michael person, but today she announced that they were engaged to be married. Mia had never met him but knew that if he had convinced Lynda Hastings to even think about getting married, she had to meet him. She seized the opportunity by inviting them to a pre-Christmas dinner. Lynda initially declined the offer and Mia thought that was somewhat strange, but chalked it up to her busy schedule. She kept saying that she didn't want her to go out of her way, but finally Mia convinced her that she would keep it really simple. She and Edward had already shopped for enough groceries to carry them through the next millennium. Everything she needed was already in her kitchen. To that, Lynda agreed to come.

With Christmas less than three days away, the days seemed to get shorter and shorter. Mia was able to work for a couple of hours on her new book about her ordeal and felt pretty good about the progress she had made on it in such little time. By four o'clock dinner was ready, all her calls had been made and she had even written out the pending bills for the month. The house was filled with the aromas of grilled petrale with lemon and butter, roasted potatoes and a steamed asparagus and carrot mixture. She put the white wine and a lemon meringue pie in the refrigerator to chill while she took a nice, long bath.

She headed upstairs to the bedroom and then remembered that she had not spoken with Edward since early this morning. She thought it might be a good idea to let him know that they were having guests in case he made plans for the evening. She picked up the phone and pressed the speed dial for Edward's office. Immediately, Nathalie answered, "Mr. Simone's office."

"Hi Nathalie, this is Mia how are you?"

"Oh, Mrs. Simone I'm fine. How are you doing?"

"Much better thank you."

"I'm so glad to hear that. I just want to say that I'm so sorry for what happened to you and that I'm very glad you're back. Edward is like a new person."

"Thank you, Nathalie. That means a lot. And, I can't tell you how glad I am to be back. I really have a deeper appreciation for life now."

"Oh, I can only imagine. Okay take care. I'll put you through to Edward now."

"Thanks."

There was a brief pause and then Edward's voice came through the line and she knew that he knew who was on the line.

"Uhmmm. Hey there sexy lady."

"Is that how you greet all your clients?"

"No, only the sexy ones."

"You better stop it. I could have been a client," Mia teased.

"Not on Nathalie's watch you couldn't."

"You're right about that. She's much too efficient to let that happen. You should really think of advancing her within the firm. I think she could go far."

"Honey, I've told her that many times. And, as much as I would hate to lose her, I would never try to hold her back. But, she said she's just not ready for all the headaches that come along with a higher level position."

"As a woman who was part of the corporate work-force, I can certainly appreciate her feelings. But, I was call-ing to let you know that we're having company for dinner this evening."

"Oh really, and whom might that be?"

"It would be Lynda and her fiancé, Michael."

"Excuse me?" Edward asked, a bit taken off guard.

"Why are you so surprised?"

"I guess I really shouldn't be. It's just that it seems so sudden," Edward admitted, feeling more surprised than he let on after thinking about the incident that took place in his living room.

Mia grinned. "Well, you heard it right here first. Her fiancé."

"Well, that was a fast courtship."

"Yes, it was. Apparently, my good friend had a big, strong shoulder to cry on while I was going through hell," Mia joked.

Edward was silent for a moment as he thought about Mia's statement. Mia really had no idea what type of friend she had and that Lynda probably never had her best interest in mind.

"You pretty busy?"

"Hmmm? Oh, a little. I didn't mean to be so dis-tracted. It's just a lot that I need to get caught up on. I'd really prefer to skip this dinner party altogether."

"Wait a minute now! First Lynda and now you?"

"What are you talking about?" Edward asked as his

heart skipped a beat.

"Well, I almost had to threaten her to get her to come over and now you're saying that you would prefer to skip dinner."

"I didn't say I was," Edward lied. "I was just thinking out loud. I'll come but I might be late, after working from home for almost two months, there's a lot to catch up on here."

"I'm sorry. I really just threw this entire thing together and didn't think about the plans others might have. If you can't come, I'll understand."

"I'll try my best, but you know this deal I'm working on could be the one that makes me partner. And, because of that, I have to be at the very top of my game. Everything has to be accurate and precise."

"I know, babe," Mia sighed. "I'll see you when you get here."

"Okay," Edward replied. "I love you," he said and quickly hung up the phone.

"I love you too," Mia responded to the dial tone. She hung up the phone and headed upstairs to take her hot bath, which had become much more needed now.

"Mmmm. Mia this is delicious," Michael said through a forkful of pie.

"I'm glad you like it. I got the recipe from Edward's mom. I'm really sorry that he couldn't make it, but he has this big deal he's working on. I would've loved for him to meet you."

"Yeah, it's too bad. Who knows how many more opportunities like these we'll get."

Mia was caught off guard by the statement. "What does that mean?" she asked almost too defensively.

"I'm sorry," Michael said as he looked up at the

two women with obvious embarrassment.

"Don't be sorry," Lynda interjected. "I didn't tell her yet."

Mia let out an exasperated sigh and glanced back and forth between the two.

"Okay you two. That's it. What's going on?"

"Well, we're moving to New York," Lynda said sheepishly.

"Oh, my goodness," Mia gasped. "When?"

"In the next two to three months."

"Wow. You two aren't wasting any time are you? I mean gee whiz, when is the wedding?"

"June. I've always wanted to be a June bride."

Mia raised a finely arched eyebrow in her friend's direction. "Look's like you have a lot to do in the next six months."

"Yeah," Lynda agreed, avoiding direct eye contact with her friend.

Just then, Edward walked in to the formal dining room. "Hello everyone. Sorry I'm late." He and Lynda exchanged an awkward handshake.

"Hi honey." Mia stood and kissed Edward on the cheek. "This is Michael Bledsoe, Lynda's fiancé."

Edward extended his hand to shake Michael's, "Nice to meet you man. Heard a lot about you."

"Same here," Michael said returning a warm handshake.

Edward took a seat and Mia stood to heat a plate for him. "Oh, no that's okay, babe. I'll get it."

When Edward returned, Mia said, "So, honey. Big news. Lynda and Michael are getting married in June and they're moving to New York."

"Well, that is big news," Edward said as he cut into the tender fish. "At least now you'll have someone to visit and shop with when you're there touring."

"That's right," Lynda added.

Mia was silent for a moment and then looking around as if she'd just come out of a daze, she said, "I'm going to clear some of these dishes."

"I'll help," Lynda offercd. "You two talk business and we'll be back in a sec."

When the two women were in the kitchen, Mia turned to Lynda with concern in her eyes, "Lynda, what's going on? I know we've been out of touch for a couple of months, but this really isn't like you. I'm sensing something deeper than what I see and hear. Why so drastic a move so soon?"

Lynda's eyes filled with tears as her mind flashed to how she'd betrayed her friend. The truth was that she had written Mia off as being dead almost from the moment she learned of her disappearance. She knew now the reason for her actions with Edward and because of that, she knew that she could never be friends with Mia, not the way they had been. When Michael suggested moving to New York, it just seemed the right thing to do. Away from what she wanted, but would never have—Edward. Away from the guilt and the person she had betrayed, but could never let know—Mia.

"Because it's time, Mia," she responded slowly. "When you were gone," she continued. " I realized how lonely my existence really was. Michael was there and filled a major void."

"But—" Mia started.

"No, let me finish," Lynda cut her off. "In the process, I learned something about myself and that is that I've been afraid to venture out because of being scorned so many times. Secretly, I've been living the relationship I would like to have, vicariously through you and Edward. Michael has been a prince and has brought forth feelings in me that I didn't know existed. And, to tell you the truth, I'm not getting any younger."

Mia stood speechless, trying to find the words to respond to the revelation she'd just learned. Words simply escaped her.

"Lynda, I-I-didn't know. I'm so sorry."

"No, there is no need for you to apologize. These are my issues."

"Well, I'm happy that you've found someone to love and if there's anything I can do to help with any of your wedding or moving plans, please let me know."

"There is one thing. Can you please be my matron of honor?"

"I would be honored."

"I appreciate that, Mia. I really do. You're a very good friend and I'm going to miss you."

"I'm going to miss you too.

The two women hugged, knowing that their friendship had changed forever.

Mia and Edward relaxed in their large four-poster bed. The evening had ended with the exchange of simple pleasantries, but by that time Mia was convinced that her little dinner party hadn't been such a great idea. Mia lay staring into space.

"Penny for your thoughts," Edward said, interrupting her introspection.

"You certainly wouldn't become rich."

Edward laughed heartily. His laughter was contagious and Mia had to smile.

"No, I'm serious," she said returning to her gloomy state.

"Look babe, I know that this get-together didn't turn out how you planned. I guess I would be upset too if my best friend were moving to another state. But, you have to respect that Lynda is a grown woman who knows what's best for her."

"I do respect that, it's just the way she went about

it. I mean, I thought we were so much closer than that. It seems like she just forgot about me when I was gone and that really kinda hurts."

Edward put his arm around Mia and drew her near him. She sighed, inhaling the scent of his cologne and listening to his heartbeat. In his arms had always made her feel protected from the world and now was no different.

"You know, I'm not trying to make light of your friendship, but sometimes tragedy can reveal the truth about relationships. And, the fact is, friends can come and go, but I'm here to stay."

Mia smirked, "Did you get that from a Hallmark card or what?"

"No that one is compliments of me."

"Yeah, I thought so." Mia paused, "But, I know you're right and I guess that's why it's so hard to accept."

"Well try accepting this." Edward trailed light kisses along Mia's forehead down to her lips, where he captured her mouth with his. His hand slowly traveled the length of her thigh and across the soft fabric of her silk nightie up to one of her full breasts. It was there that he stopped and fingered the erect nipple before suckling it like the sweetest fruit he'd ever tasted. Mia moaned as he massaged and suckled both her breasts in a hungry, lustful manner. They had not made love since Mia returned home almost three months ago. Edward wanted to make sure that she was ready, that she wanted it as much as he did. He knew now that waiting had been a good idea. As he slowly slid the gown off Mia, where it came to rest on the floor, he observed the way Mia's body responded to his every touch.

Mia's breath caught in her throat and she was reminded of being on a ride at the amusement park. The thrill, anticipation and tingling sensation in her stomach all gave way to an ecstasy she didn't realize she missed so much, until now. Edward had been very patient with her over the past couple of months and she knew it had probably not been easy for him. But, the time had not been right. Between her suffering from nightmares and convalescing from broken bones, the weeks had flown by. But she was sure that the wait would be more than worthwhile.

Edward massaged, licked and caressed every part of Mia's body until her nerve endings were on fire. She begged him for what they both had been waiting for, no longer able to endure his lengthy foreplay. When he entered her, it was the most exquisite, blissful feeling she had ever known. She shuddered, moaned and then opened her eyes. Edward's lustful gaze held hers as he whispered, "I love you."

Mia was unable to speak as she was caught up in the rapture of the moment, her mind floating on a sexual journey which far surpassed her current physical pleasure. Edward moved with fluid, experienced movements as he explored the concavity of his wife. He savored the essence of every moment, taking himself and Mia to new heights. Just when Mia thought they were about to reach the pinnacle of their lovemaking, without missing a beat, Edward expertly flipped them both over. As she straddled him, he continued to massage her breasts, neck and buttocks. He then rose to face her, gaining further entry into her heated walls, his throbbing member pulsing in unison with his heartbeat. Regaining their rhythm, they quickly ascended to a new, unbearable crescendo. Sweat streamed from Mia's face, down her neck and in between her breasts as she panted and moaned in sheer delight. When neither of them could no longer restrain the unbridled passion that held them together, Edward's kisses became urgent and hungry. Mia held on digging her nails into the smooth, firm skin of his back. Together, their minds, bodies and spirits fused together as if condoning their union. It symbolized an infinite bond that would surpass all time, space, friendships and tragedies.

Chapter Twenty-Three

"Well that was a beautiful wedding," Mia sighed as she looked out the airplane window at the blacktop that soon became a blur.

"Yes it was," Edward assented. He looked at her out of the corner of his eye.

"Yeah. I just know it's not the same anymore."

"What do you mean. She thought enough of you to have you be her matron of honor, didn't she?"

"Sure. All in all a great send-off don't you think?"

"What I think is that you're blowing this way out of proportion. Mia, there are such things as long-distance friendships you know. And you have a full life with a career that most women would kill for."

Mia snickered. "And what about my husband?"

"Well, that goes without saying."

Mia pinched him on his arm and laughed as he wriggled in his seat.

"I know, honey. I thought I was adult enough to be over this and to go to the wedding and come back unaffected. But I have to tell you, I think this is so hard for me because instead of farewell, it's really good-bye."

"It's only good-bye if you make it. Mia, bottom line, you just have to accept that your friend has moved on," Edward said with an edge to his voice.

As the plane made its descent into LAX, Mia began to feel sick to her stomach. She felt like she was on a ship rather than a plane. Suddenly, sweat beaded her brow and upper lip and she fought down the bile that burned in her throat. Swallowing hard to keep the nausea at bay, she regained her bearings and gathered her belonging to exit the plane. As they walked through the terminal, Mia was stricken with another wave of nausea. She dropped her luggage and raced through the crowds of people to the nearest ladies room.

Edward stood dumbfounded, not knowing whether to rush in behind her or stay where he was. Within moments, Mia re-appeared with a flushed face and sweaty appearance.

"Are you okay, babe?"

"I feel a little better now," she replied weakly. "I just don't know what came over me."

"We need to get you home. Maybe this trip has just been too much for you."

"I think so," Mia agreed as Edward wrapped a supportive arm around her waist and helped her through the terminal.

"Mia, I think you need to go to the doctor. You've been vomiting for three days now," Edward said as Mia slowly made her way back to the bed from the restroom.

"No, it's probably just the flu or some bug I caught while we were away," Mia croaked as she climbed back under the comforter.

"Please don't lay there and give me your self-diagnosis. At this rate, you'll be dehydrated by the end of the day," he barked as he picked up the phone and pressed the speed dial button to Mia's doctor. "Yes, hi. I'd like to make an appointment for Mia Simone. Your earliest appointment would be great. Fine. Thank you."

"Don't you have to be at work?" Mia asked.

Edward gave Mia an impatient look as he walked over to the armoire and pulled a pair of sweats and a T-shirt out for Mia. "We have to be there in twenty minutes. I'll go in to work after I have you situated."

###

"Are you sure you feel well enough to be left alone," Edward asked, concern etched across his handsome features.

"I'm sure. That electrolyte solution seems to have settled my stomach some. I feel a lot better already," Mia replied as they stood in the foyer removing her coat.

"So they'll have the results of your blood work sometime today?" Edward asked as he helped Mia up the stairs and into the bed.

"Yeah, they said before five o'clock I should receive a call."

"Okay, you try and get some rest," he said kissing her on the forehead. "I'm going to put the phone here. I wouldn't even go in if I didn't have this meeting with the partners regarding this acquisition, but you call and have Nathalie interrupt me if you need anything, okay?"

"I promise," Mia agreed groggily.

"I should be home by five-thirty."

###

Edward had twenty minutes to make it to his meeting with Kincaid and Blake, but he'd be lucky if he made it there in forty minutes. Traffic crawled along the highway on this muggy, Friday afternoon. He pressed the speed-dial button on his car phone and immediately, Nathalie answered, "Edward Simone's office."

"Nathalie, it's Edward."

"Hi, are you on your way in?"

"Yes and caught in traffic. Please let Kincaid and Blake know I'm running about twenty minutes late."

"Will do, is there anything else?"

"Yes, pull the Webber file and have it ready for me when I get there."

Edward arrived to the office thirty minutes late for his meeting. He cursed all the way up on the elevator. He couldn't remember the last time he was late for a meeting. Any idiot knew you didn't show up late for a meeting with the partners of your company. He had blown off a major presentation that he was to present to them a couple of months ago, but of course everyone understood that. Today might serve as a blemish on his pristine record with them.

He raced into his office, pulled off his jacket and threw it over his guest chair. As he turned to exit his office, Nathalie was waiting at his door with the Webber file in hand. On the fly, he gave her a brisk 'thanks' and hurried down the corridor.

Kincaid and Blake were casually conversing when Edward reached the office. Out of respect, he lightly tapped on the door and poked his head in. Mr. Kincaid motioned for him to come in and have a seat. Out of nowhere, Mr. Kincaid's assistant eased the door shut behind Edward.

"Sorry I'm late, I had to take my wife to the doctor and then I got hung up in traffic."

"No explanation required, we can appreciate what you've been through over the past several months," Mr. Blake offered.

"Let me just get straight to the point, Edward. Mr. Blake and I were very impressed with the work and five year projectory you've done on the Webber acquisition."

"Thank you both very much," Edward responded as he carefully eyed both of the elderly gentlemen.

"As well as the job you've done for the firm as a whole," Mr. Blake offered.

"And so, we'd like to offer you the position of junior partner with the firm," Mr. Kincaid said smiling, revealing his coffee-stained teeth."

Edward was speechless. He had known there was the possibility of this acquisition, but he didn't know it would come this soon.

"Don't jump all over this at once, son," Mr. Blake joked. "This is a good thing," he continued.

When Edward found his voice, he said, "I-I-don't know what to say, but I accept. Thank you."

"No need for thanks, son. Like I said, we were extremely impressed with the presentation that Harvey gave in your absence. With this acquisition, will come the opportunity to create several new positions. One of which will be another position at your current level of CFO. There's no place else for you to go within the corporation, but partner, because we certainly don't want to lose your genius. You've worked twice as hard as most of the people here and have definitely earned this. This also means we don't have to cut any jobs now."

"Thanks again. Kincaid, Blake & Simone. I like the sound of that," Edward said nodding his head with a big smile on his face. The three men laughed heartily.

Edward almost wrecked twice on his way home. He couldn't wait to get home and tell Mia his good news. The thought had crossed his mind to call her, but he wanted to tell her in person. Also, he hadn't spoken with her since he left her this afternoon, but assumed that she had probably slept for most of the day.

Edward walked in the house yelling, "Mia I've got great—" But was halted by the sight of Mia sitting in the living room which struck him as odd. They never sat in the living room unless they were having guests over. Mia had changed into a pair of satin pajamas and a silk robe. She wore no make-up and her hair was pulled back and twisted in a bun atop her head. Her look was complacent.

"Honey, I've got some news," she said solemnly.

Not bothering to remove his coat, Edward stooped down in front of Mia with concern in his dark, brown eyes.

"What is it Mia? Are you okay?"

"I'm pregnant," she announced and began to squeal

with laughter.

Edward chimed in and lifted Mia off her feet to hug her. "You tryin' to give me a heart attack or what?" he asked. "That's wonderful news, baby," he continued.

He kissed her full on the lips.

"Now, you were about to make an announcement of your own?" Mia asked with a raised brow.

"Oh, I think that can wait. Let's celebrate your good news first," he said as he carried her upstairs to their bedroom.

Epilogue

One year later...

"And our next luncheon keynote speaker is critically acclaimed author and motivational speaker, Mia Simone," the young lady announced.

Mia walked carefully across the stage and up to the mic as applause thundered throughout the auditorium. She adjusted the mic and placed her arms around the podium.

"Thank you. I also want to thank Patricia Steinberger, Executive Director of the wonderful organization of Women Against Violence Against Women (WAVAW). It is a magnificent institution that physically and mentally empowers women to take precautions against being victims. As many of you may already know, I was a victim of violence. But overcame it. I believe, foremost because of my strong belief in a being much greater than myself, God. Secondly because of determination, assessing my situation and remaining calm. Additionally, having taken karate classes when I was younger didn't hurt."

The crowd laughed and Mia became a little more comfortable. This was only her second motivational speaking engagement since her self-help book was released entitled, *Healing Begins Where The Victimizing Ends*. To Mia's amazement, the book had climbed to the number one best seller list in the first week of its release. It had drawn hundreds of women, spanning many different ethnicities, to learn more about self-empowerment. When speaking with the women, who attended these conferences and workshops, Mia had been touched and saddened to learn how many women had been victims and needed to connect with someone who had survived a similar experience.

Mia completed her speech and then hurried backstage to Edward, who held their son, Edward Simone, III.

"That was great, baby," Edward said kissing Mia on the cheek and handing her their son.

"Thank you. I was a lot less nervous this time, too," she replied as she covered the baby with blankets.

"Well, you'll get over that completely in no time."

"Yeah, I guess I'll have to. I received two call this morning for more speaking engagements."

Motherhood had come naturally for Mia as was demonstrated in her easy manner with their son. Edward looked on proudly and when they were ready, he escorted his family to the limo that was waiting to take them home.

The man looked on enviously as Mia held her young child. This should be my life—my family, he thought. His eyes conveyed hurt as he stood captivated by the live picture of man, woman and child. He envisioned himself the head of this family as he held the door and watched them stroll by, seemingly oblivious of his unimportant presence as a stage hand. This empowering of women crap was for the birds, he thought bitterly. Every woman he had ever known never knew what she really wanted. She said one thing, but meant another or claimed to love one person, but really loved another—they just never could admit it.

This time it would be different. He just needed more time. Maybe a little more time would do them both some good. Soon, men would look on in envy of him because he would be the man in the live picture he just saw. With renewed determination to make this family his, he looked on as the limo pulled away from the curb.

"Until we meet again, my beautiful, Mia," he whispered.

Dear Reader,

Writing Who Will Hear My Screams was a wonderful experience. I hope you enjoyed supporting Mia, fantasizing about Edward, loathing Lynda and trying to understand Parker.

The ability to breathe life into characters and mold them into people we love and love to hate is an incredible gift. It is that much more special to evoke emotions in readers that keeps them on the edge of their seats, frantically turning pages until the gripping conclusion.

Thank you all for your support. I hope you will enjoy my next book, The Purest of Pain, coming in Spring of 2002.

I love hearing from you. Feel free to continue sending me e-mail messages at www.Bayjean2@aol.com.

Blessings,

Anna

WHO WILL HEAR MY SCREAMS

WIN A TRIP TO LOS ANGELES!

Enter the

Who Will Hear My Screams

Contest!

See reverse side for details.

Name:_____

Address: _____

City: _____ State: _____

Zip Code: _____

To enter:

1. Answer the following statement:

Now that you've read Mia's story, tell us what you would have done if you were Mia!

2. Write your answer on a separate sheet of paper (in 50 words or less.)

3. Mail to:
WHO WILL HEAR MY SCREAMS CONTEST
P.O. BOX 5077
South San Francisco, CA 94083

Offer expires December 1, 2001

1. To enter, hand print you name and complete address on the official entry form (original, photocopy, or a plain piece of paper). Then, on a separate sheet of paper (no larger than 8-1/2" x 11") in 50 words or less, hand-printed or typed, complete the following statement:

**Now that you've read Who Will Hear My Screams, tell us
what you would have done if you were Mia!**

Staple your statement to your entry form and mail to: WHO WILL HEAR MY SCREAMS CONTEST, P.O. Box 5077, South San Francisco, CA 94080. Entries must be received by December 1, 2001, in order to be eligible. Not responsible for late, lost, misdirected mail or printing errors.

2. All entries will be judged by an official representative of Apex Publishing, Inc. based upon the following criteria: Originality 35%, Content 35%, Sincerity 20%, and Clarity 10%. By entering this contest entrants accept and agree to be bound to these rules and the decisions of the judges which shall be final and binding. All entries become the property of the sponsors and will not be acknowledged or returned. Each entry must be the original work of the entrant. Winners will be notified by mail and may be required to execute an affidavit of eligibility and release which must be returned within 14 days of notification or an alternate winner will be selected.

3. PRIZES: One (1) Grand Prize winner will receive round trip airfare for two people on United Airlines. Approximate retail value: $450. One (1) Second Prize winner will receive an advance copy of Anna Dennis' upcoming release entitled: THE PUREST OF PAIN. All prizes will be awarded after December 1, 2001, based upon criteria outlined above.

4. Contest open to residents of the United States and Canada 18 years of age and older, except employees and immediate families of Apex Publishing, Inc., United Airlines, its affiliates, subsidiaries, and advertising and promotion agencies. Void in FL, VT, MD, AZ, the Province of Quebec, and wherever else prohibited by law. All Federal, State, Local and Provincial laws apply. Taxes, if any, are the sole responsibility of the prize winners. Winners are responsible for any tax/fee associated per airline ticket. If required, winners consent to the use of their name and/or photos or likeness for advertising purposes without additional compensation (except where prohibited).

5. Trip is subject to availability and black out dates, and must be taken before November 15, 2002. No transfer or substitution for prizes offered. Black out dates when travel is prohibited are 4 days before/after any major U.S. holiday; 12/15-1/7, inclusive; 7/1-9/15, inclusive. Air accommodations must be taken from any United Airlines gateway. All prize winners must provide proof of citizenship.

6. For the names of the major prize winners, send a self-addressed, stamped envelope after December 1, 2001, to: WHO WILL HEAR MY SCREAMS CONTEST WINNERS, P.O. Box 5077, South San Francisco, CA 94080.

Apex Publishing, Inc.